"You're angry," Shay said miserably.

"Shocked would be the more appropriate word," he answered, sitting down next to her.

She was stung with anger. "Shocked? You? The adventurer, the sophisticate?"

His expression had softened; in his eyes Shay saw some lingering annoyance. "I wasn't casting aspersions on your moral character, Shay, so settle down."

"Then what were you doing?"

"From the moment I met you, you've been trying to keep me at a distance. You might as well have worn a sign saying 'Look, but don't touch.' Yet tonight, you—"

She couldn't bear for him to say that she'd seduced him, though it was true, in a manner of speaking. "I'm a woman of the eighties!" she broke in.

"Yes," Mitch replied wryly. "The eighteen-eighties."

"I resent that."

"Strange. That's one of the most interesting things about you. Despite what we just did, you're an innocent."

"Is that bad or good?"

"I haven't decided yet," he said, and then they made love again, this time in the light.

Dear Reader:

Romance offers us all so much. It makes us "walk on sunshine." It gives us hope. It takes us out of our own lives, encouraging us to reach out to others. Janet Dailey is fond of saying that romance is a state of mind, that it could happen anywhere. Yet nowhere does romance seem to be as good as when it happens *here*.

Starting in February 1986, Silhouette Special Edition is featuring the AMERICAN TRIBUTE—a tribute to America, where romance has never been so wonderful. For six consecutive months, one out of every six Special Editions will be an episode in the AMERICAN TRIBUTE, a portrait of the lives of six women, all from Oklahoma. Look for the first book, *Love's Haunting Refrain* by Ada Steward, as well as stories by other favorites—Jeanne Stephens, Gena Dalton, Elaine Camp and Renee Roszel. You'll know the AMERICAN TRIBUTE by its patriotic stripe under the Silhouette Special Edition border.

AMERICAN TRIBUTE—six women, six stories, starting in February.

AMERICAN TRIBUTE—one of the reasons Silhouette Special Edition is just that—Special.

The Editors at Silhouette Books

LINDA LAEL MILLER
Ragged Rainbows

Silhouette Special Edition

Published by Silhouette Books New York

America's Publisher of Contemporary Romance

For Mary Ann and Stevie, my cousins and my
first friends. I love you.

SILHOUETTE BOOKS
300 East 42nd St., New York, N.Y. 10017

ISBN: 0-373-09324-1

First Silhouette Books printing July 1986

All the characters in this book are fictitious. Any
resemblance to actual persons, living or dead, is
purely coincidental.

Printed in the U.S.A.

LINDA LAEL MILLER

lives with her characters, sharing their dreams, joys and sorrows. They become real to her, and often surprise her with their actions. When the book is done, the parting is bearable only because she knows new people are crowding around her typewriter eager to tell their stories.

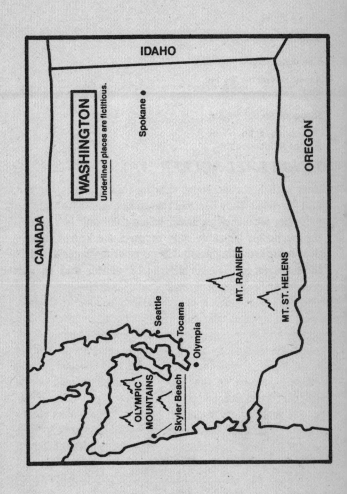

Chapter One

Marvin's toupé was slightly off-center and he was wearing his standard smile, one that promised low mileage to the public in general and headaches to Shay Kendall in particular. She sat up a little straighter in her chair and looked across the wide polished plains of her employer's desk to the view outside the window behind him. Thousands of red, yellow and blue triangular flags were snapping in the wind, a merry contrast to the cloudy coastal sky.

"I'm an office manager, Marvin," Shay said with a sigh, bringing wide hazel eyes back to his friendly face, "not an actress. While I enjoy helping plan commercials, I don't see myself in front of the camera."

"I've been promising Jeannie this trip to Europe for years," Marvin said pointedly.

Richard Barrett, a representative of an advertising agency in nearby Seattle, was leaning back against a burgeoning bookshelf, his arms folded across his chest. He was tall, with nicely cut brown hair, and would have been handsome if not for the old-fashioned horn-rimmed glasses he wore. "You're Rosamond Dallas's daughter," he put in. "Besides, I know a hundred women who would give anything for a chance like this."

Shay pushed back a lock of long, layer-cut brown hair to rub one temple with her fingers, then lifted her head, giving Mr. Barrett an ironic look. "A chance like what, Richard? You make this sound as though it's a remake of *The Ten Commandments* instead of a thirty second TV spot where I get a dump truck load of sugar poured over me and say, 'We've got a sweet deal for you at Reese Motors in Skyler Beach!' Furthermore, I fail to see what my being Rosamond's daughter has to do with anything."

Marvin was sitting back in his leather chair and smiling, probably at the image of Shay being buried under a half ton of white sugar. "There would be a sizable bonus involved, of course," he reflected aloud.

He hadn't mentioned a bonus on Friday afternoon, when he'd first presented Shay with a storyboard for a commercial starring herself rather than the infamous "Low-Margin Marvin."

Shay sighed, thinking of all the new clothes her six-year-old son, Hank, would need before school started and of the IRA account she wanted to open but couldn't afford. "How much of a bonus?" she asked, disliking Richard Barrett for the smug look that flickered briefly in his blue eyes.

Marvin named a figure that would cover the IRA payment and any amount of jeans, sneakers, jackets and T-shirts for Hank, with money left over.

"Just for one commercial? That's all I'd have to do?" Shay hated herself for wavering, but she was in no position to turn her back on so much money. While she earned a good salary working as Reese Motors's office manager and general all-around troubleshooter, it took all she could scrape together to support herself and her small son and meet the property taxes on her mother's enormous, empty house. Lord in heaven, she thought, if only someone would come along and buy that house....

Marvin and Richard exchanged indulgent looks. "If you hadn't stomped out of here on Friday," Richard said smoothly, "I would have gone on to explain that we're discussing a series of four spots, thirty seconds each. That's a lot of money for two minutes' work, Shay."

Two minutes' work. Shay was annoyed and insulted. Nobody knew better than she did that a thirty second commercial could take days to perfect; she'd fetched enough antacid tablets for Marvin and made enough conciliatory telephone calls to his wife to know. "I'm an office manager," she repeated, somewhat piteously this time.

"And a damned good one!" Marvin thundered. "I don't know what we'd have done without you all this time!"

Shay looked back over the half dozen years since she'd come to work for Marvin Reese. She had started as a receptionist and the job had been so important to her that she'd made any number of mistakes in her attempts to do it well. Marvin had been kind and his wife, Jeannie, had been a real friend, taking Shay out to lunch on occasion, helping her to find a trustworthy baby-sitter for Hank, reassuring her.

In many ways, Jeannie Reese had been a mother to Shay during those harried, scary days of new independence. Rosamond—nobody had suspected that her sudden tendency toward forgetfulness and fits of temper was the beginning of Alzheimer's disease—had been living on a *rancho* in Mexico then, with her sixth and final husband, blissfully unconcerned with her daughter's problems.

Now, sitting there in Marvin's spacious, well-appointed office, Shay felt a sting at the memory. She had telephoned her mother right after Eliott, then principal of a high school in a small town in Oregon, had absconded with the school's sizable athletic fund and left his young and decidedly pregnant wife to deal with the consequences. Rosamond had said that she'd warned Shay not to marry an older man, hadn't she, and that she would love to send money to help out but that that was impossible, since Eduardo had just bought a thoroughbred racehorse and transporting the beast all the way from Kentucky to the Yucatan peninsula had cost so much.

"Shay?"

Shay wrenched herself back to the present moment and met Marvin's fatherly gaze. She knew then that, even without the bonus check, she would have agreed to be in his commercials. He had believed in her when she had jumbled important files and spilled coffee all over his desk and made all the salesmen on the floor screaming mad by botching up their telephone messages. He had paid for the business courses she'd taken at the junior college and given her regular raises and promotions.

He was her friend.

"It's an offer I can't refuse," she said softly. It was no use asking for approval of the storyboards; Marvin's style, which had made him a virtual legend among car dealers, left no room for temperament. Three years before, at Thanksgiving, he'd dressed up as a turkey and announced to the viewing public that Reese Motors was gobbling up good trade-ins.

Marvin unearthed his telephone from piles of factory invoices and lease agreements and dialed a number. "Jeannie? Shay's going to take over the commercials for me. Dust off your passport, honey—we're going on the trip!"

Shay rose from her chair and left Marvin's office for the sanctity of her own smaller one, only to be followed by a quietly delighted Richard.

"I have three of the four storyboards ready, if you'd like to look them over," he offered.

"Why does Marvin want me to do this?" Shay complained belatedly. "Why not one of the salesmen or some actor? Your agency has access to dozens of people...."

Richard grinned. "You know that Marvin believes in the personal touch, Shay. That's what's made him so successful. You should be proud; he must regard you as practically a member of his family."

There was some truth in Richard's words—Jeannie and Marvin had no children of their own, and they had included her and Hank in many of their holiday celebrations and summer camping trips over the past six years. What would she have done without the Reeses?

She eyed the stacks of paperwork teetering in her in-basket and drew a deep breath. "I have a lot to do, Richard. If you'll excuse me—"

The intercom buzzed and Shay picked up her telephone receiver. "Yes, Ivy? What is it?"

Ivy Prescott's voice came over the line. "Shay, that new salesman Mike hired last Tuesday is...well, he's doing something very weird."

Shay closed her eyes tightly, opened them again. With one hand, she opened the top drawer of her desk and rummaged for a bottle of aspirin, and failed to find it. "What, exactly, is he doing?"

"He's standing in the front seat of that '65 Corvette we got in last month, making a speech."

"Standing—"

"It's a convertible," Ivy broke in helpfully.

Shay made note of the fact that Richard was still loitering inside her office door and her irritation redoubled. "Good Lord. Where is Mike? He's the floor manager and this is his problem!"

"He's out sick today," Ivy answered, and there was a note of panic in her normally bright voice. "Shay, what do I do? I don't think we should bother Mr. Reese with this, his heart, you know. Oh, I wish Todd were here!"

"I'll handle it," Shay said shortly, hanging up the receiver and striding out of the office, with Richard right behind her. As she passed Ivy's desk, she gave the young receptionist a look that, judging by the heightened color in her face, conveyed what Shay thought of the idea of hiding behind Todd Simmons, Ivy's fiancé, just because he was a man.

Shay was wearing jeans and a blue cotton blouse that day, and her sneakers made a squeaky sound on the metal steps leading down into the showrooms. She smiled faintly at the customers browsing among glistening new cars as she crossed the display floor and stepped out onto the lot. Sure enough, there was a crowd gathered around the recently acquired Corvette.

She pushed her way between two of the newer salesmen, drew a deep breath and addressed the wild-eyed young man standing in the driver's seat of the sports car. "Get down from there immediately," she said in a clear voice, having no idea in the world what she would do if he refused.

Remarkably, the orator ceased his discourse and got out of the car to stand facing Shay. He was red with conviction and at least one coffee break cocktail, and there was a blue stain on the pocket of his short-sleeved white shirt where his pen had leaked. "I was only—" he began.

Shay cut him off swiftly. "My office. Now."

The errant salesman followed along behind Shay as she walked back into the building, through the showroom and up the stairs. Once they were inside her office, he became petulant and not a little rebellious. "No woman orders me around," he muttered. Shay sat down in her chair, folded her hands in her lap so that—she glanced subtly at his name tag—Ray Metcalf wouldn't see that they were trembling just a little. "This woman, Mr. Metcalf, is ordering you out, not around. If you have any commissions coming, they will be mailed to you."

"You're firing me?" Metcalf looked stunned. He was young and uncertain of himself and it was obvious, of course, that he had a problem. Did he have a family to support?

"Yes," Shay answered firmly.

"You can't do that!"

"I can and I have. Good day, Mr. Metcalf, and good luck."

Metcalf flushed and, for a moment, the look in his eyes was ominous. Shay was a little scared, but she refused to be intimidated, meeting the man's contemptuous glare with a level gaze of her own. He turned and left the office, slamming the door behind him, and Shay let out a long breath in relief. When Ivy bounced in, moments later, she was going over a printout listing sales figures for the month before.

Despite the difference in their ages—Ivy was only twenty while Shay was nine years older—the two women were good friends. Ivy was going to marry Todd Simmons, an up-and-coming young real-estate broker, at Christmas, and Shay would be her matron of honor.

"Todd's taking me out to lunch," Ivy said, and her chin-length blond hair glistened even in the harsh fluorescent lighting of the office. "You're welcome to come along if you'd like."

"How romantic," Shay replied, with a wry twist of her lips, and went on working. "Just the three of us."

Ivy persisted. "Actually, there wouldn't be three of us. There's someone I want you to meet."

Shay laid down her pen and gave her friend a look. "Are you matchmaking again? Ivy, I've told you time and time again—"

"But this man is different."

Shay pretended to assess Ivy's dress size, which, because she was so tiny, would be petite. "I wonder if Marvin still has that turkey suit at home. With a few alterations, my dear, it might fit you. Why didn't I think of this before?" She paused for effect. "I could pull rank on you. How would you like to appear in four television commercials?"

Ivy rolled her blue-green eyes and backed out of the office, closing the door on a number of very interesting possibilities. Shay smiled to herself and went back to work.

The house was a sprawling Tudor mansion perched on a cliff overlooking the Pacific, and it was too damned big for one single, solitary man.

The dining room was formal, lit by two shimmering crystal chandeliers, and there were French doors opening onto a garden filled with pink, white, scarlet and lavender rhododendrons. The walls of the massive library were lined with handcrafted shelves and the fireplaces on the first floor were all large enough for a man to stand upright inside. The master bedroom boasted a checkerboard of tinted and clear skylights, its own hot tub lined with exquisitely painted tiles, and a broad terrace. Yes, the place was definitely too big and too fancy.

"I'll take it," Mitch Prescott said, leaning against the redwood railing of the upstairs terrace. The salt breeze rippled gently through his dark blond hair and the sound of the incoming tide, far below, was a soothing song.

Todd Simmons, soon to be Mitch's brother-in-law, looked pleased, as well he might, considering the commission his fledgling real-estate firm would collect on the sale. Mitch noticed that Todd's hand trembled a little as he extended it to seal the agreement.

Inwardly, Mitch was wondering what had possessed him to meet the outrageous asking price on this monster of a house within fifteen minutes of walking through the front door. He decided that he'd done it for Ivy, his half-sister. Since she was going to marry Simmons, the sale would benefit her, too.

"When can I move in?" Mitch asked, resting against the railing again and gazing far out to sea. His hotel room was comfortable, but he had spent too much of his life in places like it; he wanted to live in a real house.

"Now, if you'd like," Simmons answered promptly. He seemed to vibrate with suppressed excitement, as though he'd like to jump up in the air and kick his heels together. "In this case, the closing will be little more than a formality. I don't mind telling you that Rosamond Dallas's daughter is anxious to unload the place."

The famous name dropped on Mitch's weary mind with all the grace of a boxcar tumbling into a ravine. "I thought Miss Dallas was dead," he ventured.

A sad expression moved in Todd's eyes as he shook his head and drew a package of gum from the pocket of his blue sports jacket. He was good-looking, with dark hair and a solid build; he and Ivy would have beautiful children.

"Rosamond has Alzheimer's disease," he said, and he gave a long sigh before going on. "It's a shame, isn't it? She made all those great movies, married all those men, bought this house and half a dozen others just as impressive all over the United States, and she winds up staring at the walls over at Seaview Convalescent, with the whole world thinking she's dead. The hell of it is, she's only forty-seven."

"My God," Mitch whispered. He was thirty-seven himself; it was sobering to imagine having just ten good years left. Rosamond, at his age, had been at the height of her powers.

Todd ran a hand through his dark hair and worked up a grin. "Things change," he said philosophically. "Time moves on. Rosamond doesn't have any use for a house like this now, and the taxes have been a nightmare for her daughter."

Mitch was already thinking like a journalist, even though he'd sworn that he wouldn't write again for at least a year. He was in the beginning stages of burnout, he had told his agent just that morning. He'd asked Ivan to get him an extension on his current contract, in fact. Now, six hours later, here he was thinking in terms of outlines and research material. "Rosamond Dallas must have earned millions, Todd. She was a star in every sense of the word. Why would the taxes on this place put a strain on anybody in her family?"

Todd unwrapped the stick of gum, folded it, accordion-fashion, into his mouth and tucked the papers into his pocket. "Rosamond had six husbands," he answered after a moment or two of sad reflection. "Except for Riley Thompson—he's a country and western singer and pays for her care over at Seaview—they were all jerks with a talent for picking the worst investments and the slowest horses."

"But the profit from selling this house—"

"That will go to clear up the last of Rosamond's personal debts. Shay won't see a dime of it."

"Shay. The daughter?"

Todd nodded. "You'll meet her tonight. She's Ivy's best friend, works for Marvin Reese."

Mitch couldn't help smiling at the mention of Reese, even though he was depressed that someone could make a mark on the world the way Rosamond Dallas had and have nothing more to pass on to her daughter than a pile of debts. Ivy had written him often about her employer, who was something of a local celebrity and the owner of one of the largest new-and-used car operations in the state of Washington. Television commercials were Reese's claim to fame; he had a real gift for the ridiculous.

Mitch's smile faded away. "Did Shay grow up in this house, by any chance?" he asked. He couldn't think why the answer should interest him, but it did.

"Like a lot of show people, Rosamond was something of a vagabond. Shay lived here when she was a little girl, on and off. Later, she spent a lot of time in Swiss boarding schools. Went to college for a couple of years, somewhere in Oregon, and that's when she met—" Todd paused and looked sheepish. "Damn, I've said too much and probably bored you to death in the process. I should be talking about the house. I can have the papers ready by tonight, and I'll leave my keys with you."

He removed several labeled keys from a ring choked with similar ones and they clinked as they fell into Mitch's palm. "Ivy mentioned dinner, didn't she? You'll be our guest, of course."

Mitch nodded. Todd thanked him, shook his hand again and left.

When he was alone, Mitch went outside to explore the grounds, wondering at himself. He hadn't intended to settle down. Certainly he hadn't intended to buy a house. He had come to town to see Ivy and meet her future husband, to relax and maybe fish and sail a little, and he'd agreed to look at this house only because he'd been intrigued by his sister's descriptions of it.

Out back he discovered an old-fashioned gazebo, almost hidden in tangles of climbing rosebushes. Pungently fragrant pink and yellow blossoms nodded in the dull, late morning sunshine, serenaded by bees. The realization that he would have to hire a gardener as well as a housekeeper made Mitch shake his head.

He rounded the gazebo and found another surprise, a little girl's playhouse, painted white. The miniature structure was perfectly proportioned, with real cedar shingles on the roof and green shutters at the windows. Mitch Prescott, hunter of Nazi war criminals, infiltrator of half a dozen chapters of the Ku Klux Klan, trusted confidant of Colombian cocaine dealers, was enchanted.

He stepped nearer the playhouse. The paint was peeling and the shingles were loose and there were, he could see through the lilliputian front window, repairs to be made on the inside as well. Still, he smiled to imagine how Kelly, his seven-year-old daughter, would love to play here, in this strangely magical place, spinning the dreams and fantasies that came so easily to children.

Shay stormed out of Marvin's office muttering, barely noticing Ivy, who sat at her computer terminal in the center of the reception room. "Bees...a half-ton of sugar...that could kill me...."

"Todd sold the house!" Ivy blurted as Shay fumbled for the knob on her office door.

She stopped cold, the storyboards for the outrageous commercials under one arm, and stared at Ivy, at once alarmed and hopeful. "Which house?" she asked in a voice just above a whisper.

Ivy's aquamarine eyes were shining and her elegant cheekbones were tinted pink. "Yours—I mean, your mother's. Oh, Shay, isn't it wonderful? You'll be able to clear up all those bills and Todd will make the biggest commission ever!"

Shay forgot her intention to lock herself up in her office and wallow in remorse for the rest of the afternoon. She set the storyboards aside and groped with a tremulous hand for a chair to draw up to Ivy's desk. Of course she had been anxious to see that wonderful, magnificent burden of a house sold, but the reality filled her with a curious sense of sadness and loss. "Who bought it? Who could have come up with that kind of money?" she asked, speaking more to the cosmos than to Ivy.

Her friend sat up very straight in her chair and beamed proudly. "My brother, Mitch."

Shay had a headache. She pulled in a steadying breath and tried to remember all that Ivy had told her, over the years, about her brother. He and Ivy did not share the same mother; in fact, Mitch and his stepmother avoided each other as much as possible. Shay had had the impression that Mitch Prescott was very successful, in some nebulous and unconventional way, and she remembered that he had once been married and had a child, a little girl if she remembered correctly. Probably because of the rift between himself and Ivy's mother, he had rarely been to Skyler Beach.

Ivy looked as though she would burst. "I knew Mitch would want that house, if I could just get him to look at it," she confided happily. But then she peered at Shay, her eyes wide and a bit worried. "Shay, are you all right? You look awful!"

Shay stood up and moved like a sleepwalker toward the privacy of her office.

"Shay?" Ivy called after her. "I thought you'd be pleased. I thought—"

Shay turned in the doorway, the storyboards leaving stains of colored chalk on her jeans and her pale blue blouse. She smiled shakily and ran the fingers of her left hand through her hair, hoping the lie didn't show in her eyes.

"I am happy," she said. And then she went into the office, closed the door and hurled the storyboards across the room.

"Dinner?"

Ivy was clearly going to stand fast. "Don't you dare say no, Shay Kendall. You wanted to be free of that house and Todd sold it for you and the least you can do is let us treat you to dinner to celebrate."

Shay gathered up the last of the invoices she had been checking and put them into the basket on her desk. It had been a difficult day, what with the planning of the commercials and that salesman making his speech on the front lot. Of course, it was a blessing that the house had been sold and she was relieved to be free of the financial burden it had represented, but parting with the place was something of an emotional shock all the same. She would have preferred to spend the evening at home, lounging about with a good book and maybe feeling a little sorry for herself. "Your brother will be there, I suppose."

"Of course," Ivy replied with a shrug. "After all, he's the buyer."

Shay felt a nip of envy. What would it be like to be able to buy a house like that? For a very long time, she had nursed a secret dream of starting her own catering business and being such a smashing success that she could afford to keep the place for herself and Hank. "I have to stop by Seaview to see Rosamond on my way home," she said, hoping to avoid having dinner out. "And then, of course, there's Hank...."

"Shay."

She sighed and pushed back her desk chair to stand up. "All right, all right. I'll spend a few minutes at Seaview and get a sitter for the evening."

Ivy's lovely face was alight again. "Great!" she chimed, turning to leave Shay's office.

"Wait," Shay said firmly, stopping her friend in the doorway.

Ivy looked back over one shoulder, her pretty hair following the turn of her head in a rhythmic flow of fine gold. "What?"

"Don't get any ideas about fixing me up with your brother, Ivy, because I'm not interested. Is that clear?"

Ivy rolled her eyes. "Oh, for pity's sake!" she cried dramatically.

"I mean it, Ivy."

"Meet us at the Wharf at eight," Ivy said, and then she waltzed out, closing Shay's door behind her.

Shay locked her desk, picked up her purse and cast one last disdainful look at the storyboards propped along the back of her bookshelf before leaving. She tried to be happy about the assignment and the money it would bring in, tried to be glad that the elegant house high above the beach was no longer her responsibility, tried to look forward to a marvelous dinner at Skyler Beach's finest restaurant. But, as she drove toward Seaview Convalescent Home, it was all Shay could do to keep from pulling over to the side of road, dropping her forehead to the steering wheel and crying.

Chapter Two

Shay Kendall looked nothing like her illustrious mother, Mitch thought as he watched her enter the restaurant. No, she was far more beautiful: tall with lush brown hair that fell past her shoulders in gentle tumbles of curl, and her eyes were a blend of green and brown, flecked with gold.

She wore a simple white cotton sundress and high-heeled sandals and when Ivy introduced her and she extended her hand to Mitch, something in her touch crackled up his arm and elbowed his heart. It was a sudden, painful jolt, a Sunday punch, and Mitch was off balance. To cover this, he made a subtle production of drawing back her chair and took his time rounding the table to sit down across from her.

Ivy and Todd, having greeted Shay, were now standing in front of the lobster tank, which ran the length of one wall, eagerly choosing their dinner. Their easy laughter drifted over the muted chatter of the other guests to the table beside the window.

Shay was looking out through the glass; beyond it, spatters of fading daylight danced on an ocean tinted with the pinks and golds and deep lavenders of sunset. Her eyes followed the gulls as they swooped and dived over the water, giving their raucous cries, and a slight smile curved her lips. An overwhelming feeling of tenderness filled Mitch as he watched her.

He had to say something, start a conversation. He sliced one irate glance in Ivy's direction, feeling deserted, and then plunged in with, "Ivy tells me that the house I bought belonged to your mother."

The moderation with which Mitch spoke surprised him, considering that he could see the merest hint of rosy nipples through the whispery fabric of Shay's dress. He took a steadying gulp of the white wine Todd had ordered earlier.

The hazel eyes came reluctantly to his, flickered with pain and then inward laughter at some memory. Mitch imagined Shay as a little girl, playing in that miniature house behind the gazebo, and the picture slowed down his respiration rate.

"Yes." Her voice was soft and she tossed a wistful glance toward Ivy and Todd, who were still studying their unsuspecting prey at the lobster tanks. In that instant Shay was a woman again, however vulnerable, and Mitch was rocked by the quicksilver change in her.

He tried to transform her back into the child. "That little house in back, was that yours?"

Shay smiled and nodded. "I used to spend hours there. At the time, it was completely furnished, right down to china dishes—" She fell silent and her beautiful eyes strayed again to the water beyond the window.

"I only lived there for a few years," she finished quietly.

Mitch began to wish that he had never seen Rosamond Dallas's house, let alone bought it. He felt as though he had stolen something precious from this woman and he supposed that, in a way, he had. He was relieved when Ivy and Todd came back to the table, laughing between themselves and holding hands.

He was so handsome.

Nothing Ivy had ever said about Mitch Prescott had prepared Shay for the first jarring sight of him. He was a few inches taller than she was, with broad shoulders and hair of a toasted caramel shade, but it was his eyes that unsettled her the most. They were a deep brown, quick and brazen and tender, all at once. His hands looked strong, and they were dusted with butternut-gold hair, as was the generous expanse of chest revealed by his open-throated white shirt. He had just the suggestion of a beard and the effect was one of quiet, inexorable masculinity.

Here was a man, Shay decided uneasily, who had no self-doubts at all. He was probably arrogant.

She sat up a little straighter and tried to ignore him. His vitality stirred her in a most disturbing way. What would it be like to be caressed by those deft, confident hands?

Shay's arm trembled a little as she reached out for her wineglass. Fantasies sprang, scary and delicious, into her mind, and she battled them fiercely. God knew, she reminded herself, Eliott Kendall had taught her all she needed or wanted to know about men.

Ivy was chattering as she sat down, her eyes bright with the love she bore Todd Simmons and the excitement of having her adored brother nearby. "Aren't you going to pick out which lobster you want?" she demanded, looking from Shay to Mitch with good-natured impatience.

"I make it a point," Mitch said flatly, "never to eat anything I've seen groveling on the bottom of a fish tank. I'll have steak."

Ivy's lower lip jutted out prettily and she turned to Shay. "What about you? You're having lobster, aren't you?"

Shay grabbed for her menu and hid behind it. Why hadn't she followed her instincts and stayed home? She should have known she wouldn't be able to handle this evening, not after the day she'd had. Not after losing—*selling* the house.

"Shay?" Ivy prodded.

"I'll have lobster," Shay conceded, mostly because she couldn't make sense of the menu. She felt silly. Good Lord, she was twenty-nine years old, self-supporting, the mother of a six-year-old son, and here she was, cowering behind a hunk of plastic-covered paper.

"Well, go choose one then!"

Shay shook her head. "I'll let the waiter do that," she said lamely. I'm in no mood to sign a death warrant, she thought. Or the papers that will release that very special house to a stranger.

She lowered the menu and her eyes locked with Mitch Prescott's thoughtful gaze. She felt as though he'd bared her breasts or something, even though there was nothing objectionable in his regard. Beneath her dress her nipples tightened in response, and she felt a hot flush pool on her cheekbones.

Mitch smiled then, almost imperceptibly, and his eyes—God, she had to be imagining it, she thought—transmitted a quietly confident acknowledgment, not to mention a promise.

A wave of heat passed over Shay, so dizzying that she had to drop her eyes and grip the arms of her chair for a moment. Stop it, she said to herself. You don't even know this man.

A waiter appeared and, vaguely, Shay heard Todd ordering dinner.

Ivy startled her back to full alertness by announcing, "Shay's going to be a star. I'll bet she'll be so good that Marvin will want her to do all the commercials."

"Ivy!" Shay protested, embarrassed beyond bearing. Out of the corner of one eye she saw Mitch Prescott's mouth twitch slightly.

"What's the big secret?" Ivy complained. "Everybody in western Washington is going to see you anyway. You'll be famous."

"Or infamous," Todd teased, but his eyes were gentle. "How is your mother, Shay?"

Shay didn't like to discuss Rosamond, but the subject was infinitely preferable to having Ivy leap into a full and mortifying description of the commercials Shay would begin filming the following week, after Marvin and Jeannie departed for faraway places. "She's about the same," she said miserably.

The salads arrived and Shay pretended to be ravenous, since no one would expect her to talk with her mouth full of lettuce and house dressing. Mercifully, the conversation shifted to Todd's dream of building a series of condominiums on a stretch of property south of Skyler Beach.

Throughout dinner, Ivy chattered about her Christmas wedding, and when the plates had been removed, Todd brought out the papers that would transfer ownership of Rosamond's last grand house to Mitch. Shay signed them with a burning lump in her throat and, when Ivy and Todd went off to the lounge to dance, she moved to make her escape.

"Wait," Mitch said with gruff tenderness, and though he didn't touch Shay in any physical way, he restrained her with that one word.

She sank back into her chair, near tears. "I know I haven't been very good company. I'm sorry...."

His hand came across the table and his fingers were warm and gentle on Shay's wrist. A tingling tremor moved through her and she wanted to die because she knew Mitch had felt it and possibly guessed its meaning. "Let me take you home," he said.

For a moment Shay was tempted to accept, even though she was terrified at the thought of being alone with this particular man. "I have my car," she managed to say, and inwardly she despaired because she knew she must seem colorless and tongue-tied to Mitch and a part of her wanted very much to impress him.

He rose and pulled back her chair for her, escorted her as far as her elderly brown Toyota on the far side of the parking lot. There were deep grooves in his cheeks when he smiled at Shay's nervous efforts to open the car door. When she was finally settled behind the steering wheel, Mitch lingered, bending slightly to look through the open window, and there was an expression of bafflement in his eyes. He probably wondered why there were three arthritic French fries, a fast-food carton and one worn-out sneaker resting on the opposite seat.

"I'm sorry, Shay," he said.

"Sorry?"

"About the house. About the hard time Ivy gave you."

Shay was surprised to find herself smiling. She started the car and shifted into reverse; there was hope, after all, of making a dignified exit. "No problem," she said brightly. "I'm used to Ivy. Enjoy the house."

Mitch nodded and Shay backed up with a flourish, feeling oddly relieved and even a bit dashing. Oh, for an Isadora Duncan-style scarf to flow dramatically behind her as she swept away! She was her mother's daughter after all.

She waved at Mitch Prescott and started into the light evening traffic and the muffler fell off her car, clattering on the asphalt.

Mitch was there instantly, doing his best not to grin. Shay went from wanting to impress him to wanting to slap him across the face. The roar of the engine was deafening; she backed into the parking lot and turned off the ignition.

Without a word, Mitch opened the door and when Shay got out, he took her arm and escorted her toward a shiny foreign status symbol with a sliding sunroof and spoked wheels. The muffler wouldn't dare fall off this car.

"Where do you live?" Mitch asked reasonably.

Shay muttered directions, unable to look at him. Damn. First he'd seen her old car virtually fall apart before his eyes and now he was going to see her rented house with its sagging stoop and peeling paint. The grass out front needed cutting and the mailbox leaned to one side and the picture windows, out of keeping with the pre-World War II design, gave the place a look of wide-eyed surprise.

By the time Mitch's sleek car came to a stop in front of Shay's house, it was dark enough to cover major flaws. The screen door flew open and Hank burst into the glow of the porchlight, his teenage baby-sitter, Sally, behind him.

"Mom!" he whooped, bounding down the front walk on bare feet. "Wow! That's some awesome car!"

Shay was smiling again; her son had a way of putting things into perspective. Sagging stoop be damned. She was rich because she had Hank.

She turned to Mitch, opening her own door as she did so, and put down a foolish urge to invite him inside. "Good night, Mr. Prescott, and thank you."

He inclined his head slightly in answer and Shay felt an incomprehensible yearning to be kissed. She got out of the car and cut Hank off at the gate.

"Who was that?" the little boy wanted to know.

Shay ruffled his red-brown hair with one hand and ushered him back down the walk. "The man who bought Rosamond's house."

"Uncle Garrett called," Hank announced when they were inside.

Shay paid the baby-sitter, kicked off her high-heeled sandals and sank onto her scratchy garage-sale couch. Garrett Thompson had been her stepbrother, during Rosamond's Nashville phase, and though Shay rarely saw him, their relationship was a close one.

Hank was dancing from one foot to the other, obviously ready to burst. "Uncle Garrett called!" he repeated.

"Did he want me to call him back?" Shay asked, resting her feet on the coffee table with a sigh of relief.

Hank shook his head. "He's coming here. He bought a house you can drive and he's going fishing and he wants me to go, too!"

Shay frowned. "A house—oh. You mean a motor home."

"Yeah. Can I go with him, Mom? Please?"

"That depends, tiger. Maggie and the kids will be going, too, I suppose?"

Hank nodded and Shay felt a pang at his eagerness, even though she understood. He was a little boy, after all, and he needed masculine companionship. He adored Garrett and the feeling appeared to be mutual. "We'd be gone a whole month."

Shay closed her eyes. "We'll talk about this tomorrow, Hank," she said. "I've had a long day and I'm too tired to make any decisions."

Anxious to stay in his mother's good graces, Hank got ready for bed without being told. Shay went into his room and gave his freckled forehead a kiss. When he protested, she tickled him into a spate of sleepy giggles.

"I love you," she said moments later, from his doorway.

"Ah, Mom," he complained.

Smiling, Shay closed the door and went into her own room for baby-doll pajamas and a robe. After taking a quick bath and brushing her teeth, she was ready for bed.

She was not, however, ready for the heated fantasies that awaited her there, in that empty expanse of smooth sheets. She fell asleep imagining the weight of Mitch Prescott's body resting upon her own.

The next day was calm compared to the one before it. Shay's car had been brought to Reese Motors and repaired and she left work early in order to spend an hour with her mother before going home.

Rosamond sat near a broad window overlooking much of Skyler Beach, her thin, graceful hands folded in her lap, her long hair a stream of glistening, gray-marbled ebony tumbling down her back. On her lap she held the large rag doll Shay had bought for her six months before, when Rosamond had taken to wandering the halls of the convalescent home, day and night, sobbing that she'd lost her baby—couldn't someone please help her find her baby?

She had seemed content with the doll and even now she would clutch it close if anyone so much as glanced at it with interest, but Rosamond no longer cried or questioned or walked the halls. She was trapped inside herself forever, and there was no knowing whether or not she understood anything that happened around her.

On the off chance that some part of Rosamond was still aware, Shay visited often and talked to her mother as though nothing had changed between them. She told funny stories about Marvin and his crazy commercials and about the salesmen and about Hank.

Today there were no stories Shay wanted to tell, and she couldn't bring herself to mention that the beautiful house beside the sea, with its playhouse and its gazebo and its gardens of pastel rhododendrons, had been sold.

She stepped over the threshold of her mother's pleasant room and let the door whisk shut behind her, blessing Garrett's father, Riley Thompson, for being willing to pay Seaview's hefty rates. It was generous of him, considering that he and Rosamond had been divorced for some fifteen years.

"Hello, Mother," she said quietly.

Rosamond looked up with a familiar expression of bafflement in her wide eyes and held the doll close. She began to rock in her small cushioned chair.

Shay crossed the room and sank into another chair, facing Rosamond's. There was no resemblance between the two women; Rosamond's hair was raven-black, though streaked with gray now, and her eyes were violet, while Shay's were hazel and her hair was merely brown. As a child Shay had longed to be transformed into a mirror image of her mother.

"Mother?" she prompted, hating the silence.

Rosamond hugged the doll and rocked faster.

Shay worked up a shaky smile and her voice had a falsely bright note when she spoke again. "It's almost dinnertime. Are you getting hungry?"

There was no answer, of course. There never was. Shay talked until she could bear the sound of her own voice no longer and then kissed her mother's papery forehead and left.

The box, sitting in the middle of the sidewalk in front of Shay Kendall's house, was enormous. The name of a local appliance store was imprinted on one side and, as Mitch approached, he saw the crooked coin slot and the intriguing words, Lemmonad, Ten Sens, finger-painted above a square opening. He grinned and produced two nickels from the pocket of his jeans, dropping them through the slot.

They clinked on the sidewalk. The box jiggled a bit, curious sounds came from inside, and then a small freckled hand jutted out through the larger opening, clutching a grubby paper cup filled with lemonade.

Mitch chuckled, crouching as he accepted the cup. "How's business?"

"Vending machines don't talk, mister," replied the box.

Some poor mosquito had met his fate in the lemonade and Mitch tried to be subtle about pouring the stuff into the gutter behind him. "Is your mother home?" he asked.

"No," came the cardboard-muffled answer. "But my baby-sitter is here. She's putting gunk on her toenails."

"I see."

A face appeared where the cup of lemonade had been dispensed. "Are you the guy who brought my mom home last night?"

"Yep." Mitch extended a hand, which was immediately clasped by a smaller, stickier one. "My name is Mitch Prescott. What's yours?"

"Hank Kendall. Really, my name is Henry. Who'd want people callin' 'em Henry?"

"Who indeed?" Mitch countered, biting back another grin. "Think your mom will be home soon?"

The face filling the gap in the cardboard moved in a nod. "She visits Rosamond after work sometimes. Rosamond is weird."

"Oh? How so?"

"You're not a kidnapper or anything, are you? Mom says I'm not supposed to talk to strangers. Not ever."

"And she's right. In this case, it's safe, because I'm not a kidnapper, but, as a general rule—"

The box jiggled again and then toppled to one side, revealing a skinny little boy dressed in blue shorts and a He-Man T-shirt, along with a pitcher of lemonade and a stack of paper cups. "Rosamond doesn't talk or anything, and sometimes she sits on my mom's lap, just like I used to do when I was a little kid."

Mitch was touched. He sighed as he stood upright again. Before he could think of anything to say in reply, the screen door snapped open and the baby-sitter was mincing down the walk, trying not to spoil her mulberry toenails. At almost the same moment, Shay's Toyota wheezed to a stop behind Mitch's car.

He wished he had an excuse for being there. What the hell was he going to say to explain it? That he'd been awake all night and miserable all day because he wanted Shay Kendall in a way he had never before wanted any woman?

Mitch was wearing jeans and a dark blue sports shirt and the sight of him almost made Shay drop the bucket of take-out chicken she carried in the curve of one arm. Go away, go away, she thought. "Would you like to stay to dinner?" she asked aloud.

He looked inordinately relieved. "Sounds good," he said.

Sally wobbled, toes upturned, over to stand beside Shay. "Who's the hunk?" she asked in a stage whisper that sent color pulsing into her employer's face.

Shay stumbled through an introduction and was glad when Sally left for the day. Mitch watched her move down the sidewalk to her own gate with a grin. "I hope her toenails dry before the bones in her feet are permanently affected," he said.

"Dumb girl," Hank added, who secretly adored Sally.

The telephone was ringing as Shay led the way up the walk; Hank surged around her and bounded into the house to grab the receiver and shout, "Hello!"

"Why are you here?" Shay asked softly as Mitch opened the screen door for her.

"I don't know," he answered.

Hank was literally jumping up and down, holding the receiver out to Shay. "It's Uncle Garrett! It's Uncle Garrett!"

Shay smiled at the exuberance in her son's face, though it stung just a little, and handed the bucket of chicken to Mitch so that she could accept the call.

"Hi, Amazon," Garrett greeted her. "What's the latest?"

Shay was reassured by the familiar voice, even if it was coming from hundreds of miles away. The teasing nickname, conferred upon Shay during the adolescent years when she had been taller than Garrett, was welcome, too. "You don't want to know," she answered, thinking of the upcoming commercials and the attraction she felt toward the man standing behind her with a bucket of chicken in his arms.

Garrett laughed. "Yes, I do, but I'll get it out of you later. Right now, I want to find out if Maggie and I can borrow Hank for a month."

Shay swallowed hard. "A month?"

"Come on, mother hen. He needs to spend time with me, and you know it."

"But . . . a month."

"We've got big stuff planned, Shay. Camping. Fishing." There was a brief pause. "And two weeks at Dad's ranch."

Shay was fond of Riley Thompson; of all her six stepfathers, he had been the only one who hadn't seemed to regard her as an intruder. "How is Riley?"

"Great," Garrett answered. "You've heard his new hit, I assume. He's got a string of concerts booked and there's talk that he'll be nominated for another Grammy this year. You wouldn't mind, would you, Shay, our taking Hank to his place, I mean? Dad wants to get to know him."

"Why?"

"Because he's your kid, Amazon."

Shay felt sad, remembering how empty that big beautiful house overlooking the sea had been after Riley and Garrett had moved out. Everyone knew that the divorce had nearly destroyed Riley; he'd loved Rosamond and chances were that he loved her still. "I want you to tell him, for me, how much I appreciate all he's done for my mother. God knows what kind of place she'd have to stay in if he weren't paying the bills."

"Shay, if you need money—"

Shay could hear Hank and Mitch in the kitchen. It sounded as though they were setting the table, and Hank was chattering about his beloved Uncle Garrett, who had a house that could be "drived" just like a car.

"I don't need money," she whispered into the phone. "Don't you dare offer!"

Garrett sighed. "All right, all right. Maggie wants to talk to you."

Garrett's wife came on the line then; she was an Australian and Shay loved the sound of her voice. By the time the conversation was over, she had agreed to let Hank spend the next four weeks with the Thompsons and their two children.

She hung up, dashed away tears she could not have explained, and wandered into the kitchen, expecting to find Mitch and Hank waiting for her. The small table was clear.

"Out here, Mom!" Hank called.

Shay followed the voice onto the small patio in back. The chicken and potato salad and coleslaw had been set out on the sturdy little picnic table left behind by the last tenant, along with plates and silverware and glasses of milk.

"Do I get to go?" Hank's voice was small and breathless with hope.

Shay took her seat on the bench beside Mitch, because that was the way the table had been set, and smiled at her son. "Yes, you get to go," she answered, and the words came out hoarsely.

Hank gave a whoop of delight and then was too excited to eat. He begged to be excused so that he could go and tell his best friend, Louie, all about the forthcoming adventure.

The moment he was gone, Shay dissolved in tears. She was amazed at herself—she had not expected to cry—and still more amazed that Mitch Prescott drew her so easily into his arms and held her. There she was, blubbering all over his fancy blue sports shirt like a fool, and all he did was tangle one gentle hand in her hair and rock her back and forth.

It had been a very long time since Shay had had a shoulder to cry on, and humiliating as it was, silly as it was, it was a sweet indulgence.

Chapter Three

Tell me about Shay Kendall," Mitch said evenly, and his hand trembled a little as he poured coffee from the restaurant carafe into Ivy's cup.

Ivy grinned and lifted the steaming brew to her lips. "Are you this subtle with stool pigeons and talkative members of the Klan?"

"Damn it," Mitch retorted with terse impatience, "don't say things like that."

"Sorry," Ivy whispered, her eyes sparkling.

Mitch sat back in the vinyl booth. The small downtown restaurant was full of secretaries and businessmen and housewives with loud little kids demanding ice cream; after a second night in that cavernous house of his, he found the hubbub refreshing. "I asked about Ms. Kendall."

Ivy shrugged. "Very nice person. Terrific mother. Good office manager. Didn't you find out anything last night? You said you had dinner with Shay."

Mitch's jaw tightened, relaxed again. "She was married," he prompted.

Ivy looked very uncomfortable. "That was a long time ago. I've never met the guy."

Mitch sipped his coffee in a leisurely way and took his time before saying, "But you know all about him, don't you? You're Shay's friend."

"Her best friend," Ivy confirmed with an element of pride that said a great deal about Shay all by itself. A second later her blue eyes shifted from Mitch's face to the sidewalk just on the other side of the window and her shoulders slumped a little. "I don't like talking about Shay's private life. It seems...it seems disloyal."

He sighed. "I suppose it is," he agreed.

Ivy's eyes widened as a waitress arrived with club sandwiches, set the plates down and left. "Mitch, you wouldn't—you're not planning to write a book about Rosamond Dallas, are you?"

Mitch recalled his telephone conversation with his agent that morning and sorely regretted mentioning that the house he'd just bought had once belonged to the movie star. Ivan had jumped right on that bit of information, reminding Mitch that he was under contract for one more book and pointing out that a biography of Ms. Dallas, authorized or not, would sell faster than the presses could turn out new copies.

He braced both arms against the edge of the table and leaned toward his sister, glaring. "Why would I, a mild-mannered venture capitalist, want to write a book?"

Ivy was subdued by the reprimand, but her eyes were suspicious. "Okay, okay, I shouldn't have put it quite that way." She lowered her voice to a whisper. "Are you writing about Shay's mother or not?"

Mitch rolled his eyes. "Dammit, I don't know," he lied. The truth was that he had already agreed to do the book. Rosamond Dallas's whereabouts, long a mystery to the world in general, were now known, thanks to the thoughtless remark he'd made to Ivan. Mitch knew without being told that if he didn't undertake the project, his agent would send another writer to do it, and unless he missed his guess, that writer would be Lucetta White, a barracuda in Gucci's.

Lucetta was no lover of truth, and she made it a practice to ruin at least three careers and a marriage every day before breakfast, just to stay in top form. If she got hold of Rosamond's story, the result would be a vicious disaster of a book that would ride the major best-seller lists for months.

"Shay's husband was a coach or a teacher or something," Ivy said, jolting Mitch back to reality. "He was a lot older than she was, too. Anyway, he embezzled a small fortune from a high school in Cedar Landing, that's a little place just over the state line, in Oregon."

"And?"

"And Shay was pregnant at the time. She found out at her baby shower, if you can believe it. Somebody just walked in and said, 'guess what?' "

"My God."

"There was another woman involved, naturally."

Mitch was making mental notes; he would wait until later to ask his sister what had prompted her to divulge all this information. For the moment, he didn't want to chance breaking the flow. "Does anybody know where they are, Shay's ex-husband and this woman, I mean?"

Ivy shrugged. "Nobody cares except the police. Shay received divorce papers from somewhere in Mexico a few weeks after he left, but that was over six years ago. The creep could be anyplace by now."

"Who was the other woman?"

"Are you ready for this? It was the local librarian. Everybody thought she was so prim and proper and she turned out to be a mud wrestler at heart."

If it hadn't been for an aching sense of the humiliation Shay must have suffered over the incident, Mitch would have laughed at Ivy's description of the librarian. "Appearances are deceiving," he said.

"Are they, Mitch?" Ivy countered immediately. "I hope not, because when I look at you, I see a person I can trust."

"Why did you tell me about Shay's past, Ivy? You were dead set against it a minute ago."

Ivy lifted her chin and began methodically removing frilled toothpicks from the sections of her sandwich. "I just thought you should know why she's ... why she's shy."

Mitch wondered if "shy" was the proper word to describe Shay Kendall. Even though she'd wept in his arms the night before, on the bench of a rickety backyard picnic table, he sensed that she had a steel core. She was clearly a survivor. Hadn't she picked herself up after what must have been a devastating blow, found herself a good job, supported herself and her son? "Didn't Rosamond do anything to help Shay after Kendall took off with his mud wrestler?"

Ivy stopped chewing and swallowed, her eyes snapping. "She didn't lift a finger. Shay makes excuses for her, but I think the illustrious Ms. Dallas must have been an egotistical, self-centered bitch.''

Mitch considered that a distinct possibility, but he decided to reserve judgment until he had the facts.

After they had eaten their club sandwiches, Mitch drove his sister back to Reese Motors and her job. One hand on the inside handle of the car door, she gazed at her brother with wide, frightened eyes. ''All those things in your books, Mitch—did you really know all those terrible people?''

He had hedged enough for one day, he decided. ''Yes. And unless you want all those 'terrible people' to find out who and where I am, you'd better learn to be a little more discreet.''

Tears sparkled in Ivy's eyes and shimmered on her lower lashes. ''If anything happened to you—''

''Nothing is going to happen to me.'' How many times had he said that to Reba, his ex-wife? In the end, words hadn't been enough; she hadn't been able to live with the fears that haunted her. The divorce had at least been amicable; Reba was married again now, to a chiropractor with a flourishing practice and a suitably predictable life-style. He made a mental note to call and ask her to let Kelly come to visit for a few weeks.

Ivy didn't look reassured, but she did reach over and plant a hasty kiss on Mitch's cheek. A moment later she was scampering toward the entrance to the main showroom.

Mitch went shopping. He bought extra telephones in one store, pencils and spiral notebooks in another, steak and the makings of a salad in still another. He reflected, on his way home, that it might be time to get married again. He didn't mind cooking, but he sure as hell hated eating alone.

Shay carried a bag of groceries and several sacks containing new clothes for Hank's trip with Garrett and Maggie. She resisted an urge to kiss the top of her son's head after setting her purchases down on the kitchen table.

"How was work?" he asked, crawling onto a stool beside the breakfast bar that had, like the picture windows in the living room, been something of an architectural afterthought.

Shay groaned and rolled her eyes. "I spent most of it being fitted for costumes."

Hank was swinging his bare feet back and forth and there was an angry-looking mosquito bite on his right knee. "Costumes? What do you need costumes for? Halloween?"

Shay brought a dozen eggs, a pound of bacon and other miscellaneous items from the grocery bag. "Something similar, I'm afraid," she said ruefully. "I'm going to be doing four commercials."

Hank's feet stopped swinging and his brown eyes grew very wide. "You mean the kind of commercials Mr. Reese does? On TV?"

"Of course, on TV," Shay answered somewhat shortly. "Mr. and Mrs. Reese are going to be away, so I'll have to take Mr. Reese's place."

"Wow," Hank crowed, drawing the word out, his eyes shining with admiration. "Everybody will see you and know you're my mom! I betcha I could get a quarter for your autograph!"

A feeling of sadness washed over Shay; she recalled how people had waited for hours to ask Rosamond for her autograph. She had signed with a loopy flourish, Rosamond had, so friendly, so full of life, so certain of her place in a bright constellation of stars. Did that

same vibrant woman exist somewhere inside the Rosamond of today?

"You're thinking about your mom, aren't you?"
Hank wanted to know.

"Yes."

"Sally's mother says you should write a book about
Rosamond. If you did, we'd be rich."

Shay took a casserole prepared on one of her marathon cooking days from the small chest freezer in one
corner of the kitchen and slid it into the oven. She'd
been approached with the idea of a book before, and
she hated it. Telling Rosamond's most intimate secrets
to the world would be a betrayal of sorts, a form of ex-
ploitation, and besides, she was no writer. "Scratch that
plan, tiger," she said tightly. "There isn't going to be a
book and we're not going to be rich."

"Uncle Garrett is rich."

"Uncle Garrett is the son of a world-famous country
and western singer and a successful businessman in his
own right," Shay pointed out.

"Rosamond was famous. How come you're not
rich?"

"Because I'm not. Set the table, please."

"Sally's mother says she had a whole lot of husbands. Which one was your dad, Mom? You never talk
about your dad."

Shay made a production of washing her hands at the
sink, keeping her back to Hank. How could she explain that her father had never been Rosamond's husband at all, that he'd been the proverbial boy back
home, left behind when stardom beckoned? "I didn't
know my father," she said over the sound of running
water. In point of fact, she didn't even know his name.

Hank was busily setting out plates and silverware and plastic tumblers. "I guess we're alike that way, huh, Mom?"

Shay's eyes burned with sudden tears and she cursed Eliott Kendall for never caring enough to call or write and ask about his own son. "I guess so."

"I like that guy with the blue car."

Mitch. Shay found herself smiling. She sniffled and turned to face Hank. "I like him, too."

"Are you going to go out with him, on dates and stuff?"

"I don't know," Shay said, unsettled again. "Hey, it'll be a while until dinner is ready. How about trying on some of this stuff I bought for your camping trip? Maggie and Garrett will be here Saturday, so if I have to make any exchanges, I'd like to take care of it tonight."

The telephone rang as Shay was slicing cucumbers for a salad, and there was a peculiar jiggling in the pit of her stomach as she reached out one hand for the receiver. She hoped that the caller would be Mitch Prescott and then, at the nervous catching of her breath in her throat, hoped not.

"Shay?" The feminine voice rang like crystal chimes over the wires. "This is Jeannie Reese."

Mingled relief and disappointment made Shay's knees weak; she reached out with one foot for a stool and drew it near enough to sit upon. With the telephone receiver wedged between her ear and her shoulder, she went on slicing. "All ready for the big trip?" she asked, and her voice was as tremulous as her hands. If she didn't watch it, she'd cut herself.

"Ready as I'll ever be, I guess. We couldn't get away if it weren't for you. Shay, I'm so grateful."

"It was the least I could do," Shay replied, thinking of how frightened and alone she'd been when she had come back to Skyler Beach hoping to take refuge in her childhood home and found herself completely on her own. The Reeses had made all the difference. "What's up?"

"I know it's gauche, but I'm throwing my own going-away party. It'll be at our beach house, this Saturday night. Can I count on you to be there?"

By Saturday night, Hank would be gone. The house would be entirely too quiet and the first television commercial would be looming directly ahead. A distraction, especially one of the Reeses' elegant parties, would be welcome. "Is it formal?"

"Dress to the teeth, my dear."

Shay tossed the last of the cucumber slices into the salad bowl and started in on the scallions. Her wardrobe consisted mostly of jeans and simple blouses; she was either going to have to buy a new outfit or drag the sewing machine out of the back of her closet and make one. "What time?"

"Eight," Jeannie sang. "Ciao, darling. I've got fifty-six more people to call."

Shay grinned. "Ciao," she said, hanging up.

Almost instantly, the telephone rang again. This time the caller was Ivy. "You've heard about the party, I suppose?"

"Only seconds ago. How did you find out so fast?"

"Mrs. Reese appointed me to make some of the calls. Shay, what are you going to wear?"

"I don't know." The answer was sighed rather than spoken.

"We could hit the mall tomorrow, after work."

"No chance. I've got too much to do. It's tonight or nothing."

Ivy loved to shop and her voice was a disappointed wail. "Oh, damn! I can't turn a wheel tonight! I've got to sit right here in my apartment, calling all the Reeses' friends. Promise me you'll splurge, buy something really spectacular!"

Shay scraped a pile of chopped scallions into one hand with the blade of her knife and frowned suspiciously. "Ivy, what are you up to?"

"Up to?" Ivy echoed, all innocence.

"You know what I mean."

"No, I don't."

"You're awfully concerned, it seems to me, about how I plan to dress for the Reese party."

"I just want you to look good."

"For your brother, perhaps?"

"Shay Kendall!"

"Come on, Ivy. Come clean. He's going to be there, isn't he?"

"Well, I did suggest . . ."

Shay laughed, even though the pit of her stomach was jumping again and her heart was beating too fast. "That's what I thought. Has it occurred to you, dear, that if Mitch wanted to see me again he would call me himself?"

"He did drop in for chicken last night," Ivy reminded her friend.

Shay blushed to remember the way she had sobbed in Mitch's arms like a shattered child. She'd probably scared him off for good. "That didn't go too well. Don't get your hopes up, Ivy."

"Buy something fabulous," insisted the irrepressible Ivy. And then she rang off.

By the time Hank had paraded through the kitchen in each of his new outfits—by some miracle, only one pair of jeans would have to be returned—the casserole was finished. Mother and son sat down to eat and then, after clearing the table and leaving the dishes to soak, they went off to the mall.

Exchanging the jeans took only minutes, but Shay spent a full hour in the fabric store, checking out patterns and material. Finally, after much deliberation, she selected floaty black crepe for a pair of dressy, full-legged pants. In a boutique across the way, she bought a daring top of silver, black and pale blue sequins, holding her breath the whole while. The blouse, while gorgeous, was heavy and impractical and far too expensive. Would she even have the nerve to wear it?

Twice, on the way back to her car, Shay stopped in her tracks. What was she doing, spending this kind of money for one party? She had to return the blouse.

It was Hank who stopped her from doing just that. "You'll look real pretty in that shiny shirt, Mom," he said.

Shay drew a deep breath and marched onward to the car. Every woman needed to wear something wickedly glamorous, at least once in her life. Rosamond had owned closetfuls of such things.

The telephone was ringing when Shay entered the house, and Hank leaped for the living room extension. He was a born positive-thinker, expecting every call to bring momentous news.

"Yeah, she's here. Mom!"

Shay dropped her purchases on the couch and crossed the room to take the call. She was completely unprepared for the voice on the other end of the line, much as she'd hoped and dreaded to hear it earlier.

"You've heard about the party, I presume?" Mitch Prescott asked with that quiet gruffness that put everything feminine within Shay on instant red alert.

"Yes," she managed to answer.

"I don't think I can face it alone. How about lending me moral support?"

Shay couldn't imagine Mitch shrinking from anything, or needing moral support, but she felt a certain terrified gladness at the prospect of being asked to go to the party with him. "Being a sworn humanitarian," she teased, "I couldn't possibly refuse such a request."

His sigh of relief was an exaggerated one. "Thank you."

Shay laughed. "Were you really that afraid of a simple party?"

"No. I was afraid you'd say no. That, of course, would have been devastating to my masculine ego."

"We can't have that," Shay responded airily, glad that he couldn't see her and know that she was blushing like a high-schooler looking forward to her first prom. "The Reeses' beach house is quite a distance from town. We'd better leave at least a half an hour early."

"Seven?"

"Seven," Shay confirmed. The party, something of an obligation before, was suddenly the focal point of her existence; she was dizzy with excitement and a certain amount of chagrin that such an event could be so important to her. Shouldn't she be dreading her son's imminent departure instead of looking past it to a drive along miles and miles of moon-washed shore?

While Hank was taking his bath, under protest, Shay washed the dishes she'd left to soak and then got out her sewing machine. She was up long after midnight, adjusting the pattern and cutting out her silky, skirtlike slacks and basting them together. Finally she stumbled off to bed.

The next day was what Hank would have called "hairy." Three salesmen quit, Ivy went home sick and the people at Seaview called to say that Rosamond seemed to be in some kind of state.

"What kind of 'state'?" a harried Shay barked into the receiver of the telephone in her office.

"She's curled up in her bed," answered the young and obviously inexperienced nurse. "She's crying and calling for the baby."

"Have you called her doctor?"

"He's playing golf today."

"Oh, at his rates, that's just terrific!" Shay snapped. "You get him over there, my dear, if you have to drag him off the course. Does Mother have her doll?"

"What doll?"

"The rag doll. The one she won't be without."

"I didn't see it."

"Find it!"

"I'll call you back in a few minutes, Mrs. Kendall."

"See that you do," Shay replied in clipped tones just as Richard Barrett waltzed, unannounced, into her office.

"Bad day?"

Shay ran one hand through her already tousled hair and sank into the chair behind her desk. "Don't you know how to knock?"

Richard held up both hands in a concessionary gesture. "I'm sorry."

Shay sighed. "No, I'm sorry. I didn't mean to snap at you that way. How can I help you?"

"I just wanted to remind you that we're going to shoot the first commercial Monday morning. You've memorized the script, I assume?"

The script. If Shay hadn't had a pounding headache, she would have laughed. "I say my line and then read off this week's special used-car deals. That isn't too tough, Richard."

"I thought we might have a rehearsal tonight."

Shay shook her head. "No chance. My mother is in bad shape and I have to go straight to the convalescent home as soon as I leave here."

"After that—"

"My son is leaving on a camping trip with his uncle, Richard, and he'll be gone a month. I want to spend the evening with him."

"Shay—"

Now Shay held up her hands. "No more, Richard. You and Marvin insisted that I take this assignment and I agreed. But it will be done on my terms or not at all."

A look of annoyance flickered behind Richard's glasses. "Temperament rears its ugly head. I was mistaken about you, Shay. You're more like your mother than I thought."

The telephone began to jangle, and Ivy wasn't out front to screen the calls. Shay dismissed Richard with a hurried wave of one hand and snapped "Hello?"

A customer began listing, in irate and very voluble terms, all the things that were wrong with the used car he'd bought the week before. While Shay tried to address the complaint, the other lines on her telephone lit up, all blinking at once.

It was nearly seven o'clock when Shay finally got home, and she had such a headache that she gave Hank an emergency TV dinner for supper, swallowed two aspirin and collapsed into bed.

Bright and early on Saturday morning, Garrett and his family arrived in a motor home more luxuriously appointed than many houses. While Maggie stayed behind with her own children and Hank, Shay and Garrett drove to Seaview to visit Rosamond.

Because the doll had been recovered, Rosamond was no longer curled up in her bed weeping piteously for her "baby." Still, Garrett's shock at seeing a woman he undoubtedly remembered as glamorous and flippant staring vacantly off into space showed in his darkly handsome face and the widening of his steel-gray eyes.

"My God," he whispered.

Rosamond lifted her chin—she was sitting, as always, in the chair beside the window, the rag doll in her lap—at the sound of his voice. Her once-magical violet eyes widened and she surprised both her visitors by muttering, "Riley?"

Shay sank back against the wall beside the door. "No, Mother. This is—"

Garrett silenced her with a gesture of one hand, approached Rosamond and crouched before her chair. Shay realized then how much he actually resembled his father, the Riley Thompson Rosamond would remember and recognize. He stretched to kiss a faded alabaster forehead and smiled. "Hello, Roz," he said.

The bewildered joy in Rosamond's face made Shay ache inside. "Riley," she said again.

Garrett nodded and caught both his former stepmother's hands in his own strong, sun-browned ones. "How are you?" he asked softly.

Tears were stinging Shay's eyes, half blinding her. Through them, she saw Rosamond hold out the doll for Garrett to see and touch. "Baby," she said proudly.

As Garrett acknowledged the doll with a nod and a smile, Shay whirled away, unable to bear the scene any longer. She fled the room for the small bathroom adjoining it and stood there, trembling and pale, battling the false hopes that Rosamond's rare moments of lucidity always stirred in her.

When she was composed enough to come out, Rosamond had retreated back into herself; she was rocking in her chair, her lips curved into a secretive smile, the doll in her arms. Garrett wrapped a supportive arm around Shay's waist and led her out of the room into the hallway, where he gave her a brotherly kiss on the forehead.

"Poor baby," he said, and then he held Shay close and rocked her back and forth in his arms. She didn't notice the man standing at the reception desk, watching with a frown on his face.

Chapter Four

When Hank disappeared into Garrett and Maggie's sleek motor home, a lump the size of a walnut took shape in Shay's throat. He was only six; too young to be away from home for a whole month!

Garrett grinned and kissed Shay's forehead. "Relax," he urged. "Maggie and I will take good care of the boy. I promise."

Shay nodded, determined not to be a clinging, neurotic mother. Six or sixty, she reminded herself, Hank was a person in his own right and he needed experiences like this one to grow.

Briefly, Garrett caressed Shay's cheek. "Go in there and get yourself ready for that party, Amazon," he said. "Paint your toenails and slather your face with gunk. Soak in a bubble bath."

Shay couldn't help grinning. "You're just full of suggestions, aren't you?"

Garrett was serious. "Devote some time to yourself, Shay. Forget about Roz for a while and let Maggie and me worry about Hank."

It was good advice and Shay meant to heed it. After the motor home had pulled away, a happy chorus of farewell echoing behind, she went back into the house, turned on the stereo, pinned up her hair and got out the crepe trousers she'd made for the party. After hemming them, she hurried through the routine housework and then spent the rest of the morning pampering herself.

She showered and shampooed, she pedicured and manicured, she gave herself a facial. After a light luncheon consumed in blissful silence, she crawled into bed and took a long nap.

Upon rising, Shay made a chicken salad sandwich and took her time eating it. Following that, she put on her makeup, her new crepe slacks and the lovely, shimmering sequined top. She brushed her hair and worked it into a loose Gibson-girl style and put on chunky silver earrings. Looking into her bedroom mirror, she was stunned. Was this lush and glittering creature really Shay Kendall, mother of Hank, purveyor of "previously owned" autos, wearer of jeans and clear fingernail polish?

It was. Shay whirled once, delighted. It was!

Promptly at seven, Mitch arrived. He wore a pearl-gray, three-piece suit, expertly fitted, and the effect was at once rugged and Madison Avenue elegant. He was clean shaven and the scent of his cologne was crisply masculine. His brown eyes warmed as they swept over Shay, and the familiar grooves dented his cheeks when he smiled.

"Wow," he said.

Shay was glad that it was time to leave for the Reeses' beach house; she had rarely dated in the six years since her divorce and she was out of practice when it came to amenities like playing soft music and serving chilled wine and making small talk. "Wow, yourself," she said, because that was what she would have said to Hank and it came out automatically. She could have bitten her tongue.

Mitch laughed and handed her a small florist's box. There was a pink orchid inside, delicate and fragile and so exotically beautiful that Shay's eyes widened at the sight of it. It was attached to a slender band of silver elastic and she slid it onto her wrist.

"Thank you," she said.

Mitch put a gentlemanly hand to the small of her back and steered her toward the door. "Thank you," he countered huskily, and though Shay wondered what he was thanking her for, she didn't dare ask.

As his fancy car slipped away from the curb, Mitch pressed a button to expel the tape that had been blaring a Linda Ronstadt torch song.

The drive south along the coastal highway was a pleasant one. The sunset played gloriously over the rippling curl of the evening tide and the conversation was comfortable. Mitch talked about his seven-year-old daughter, Kelly, who was into Cabbage Patch Kids and ballet lessons, and Shay talked about Hank.

She wanted to ask about Mitch's ex-wife, but then he might ask about Eliott and she wasn't prepared to discuss that part of her life. It was possible, of course, Shay knew, that Ivy had told him already.

"Have you started furnishing the house yet?" Shay asked when they'd exhausted the subject of children.

Mitch shook his head and the warm humor in his eyes cooled a little, it seemed to Shay, as he glanced at her and then turned his attention back to the highway. "Not yet."

Shay was stung by his sudden reticence, and she was confused, too. "Did I say something wrong?"

"No," came the immediate response, and Mitch flung one sheepish grin in Shay's direction. "I was just having an attack of male ego, I guess."

Intrigued, Shay turned in her seat and asked, "What?"

"It isn't important."

"I think maybe it is," Shay persisted.

"I don't have the right to wonder, let alone ask."

"Ask anyway." Suddenly, Shay was nervous.

"Who is that guy who was holding you in the hallway at Seaview this morning?" The question was blurted, however reluctantly, and Shay's anxieties fled—except for one.

"That was Garrett Thompson. His father was married to my mother at one time." Shay folded her hands in her lap and drew a deep breath. "What were you doing at Seaview?"

The Reeses' beach house was in sight and Mitch looked longingly toward it, but he pulled off the highway and turned to face Shay directly. "I was asking about your mother," he said.

Shay had been braced for a lie and now, in the face of a blunt truth, she didn't know how to react. "Why?" she asked after several moments of silence.

"I don't think this is a good time to talk, Shay," Mitch replied. "Anyway, it isn't anything you need to worry about."

"But—"

His hand closed, warm and reassuring, over hers. "Trust me, okay? I promise that we'll talk after the party."

Mitch had been forthright; he could have lied about his reason for visiting Seaview, but he hadn't. Shay had no cause to distrust him. And yet the words "trust me" troubled her; it didn't matter that Mitch had spoken them: she heard them in Eliott's voice. "After the party," she said tightly.

Moments later she and Mitch entered the Reeses' spacious two-story beach house. It was a beautiful place with polished oak floors and beamed ceilings and a massive stone fireplace, and it was crowded with people.

Marvin took one look at Shay's sequined blouse and bounded away, only to return moments later wearing a pair of grossly oversized sunglasses that he'd used in a past commercial. Shay laughed and shook her head.

"I hope his tie doesn't squirt grape juice," Mitch commented in a discreet whisper.

Shay watched fondly as Marvin turned away to rejoin the party. "Don't let him fool you," she replied. "He reads Proust and Milton and speaks two languages other than English."

Mitch was still pondering this enlightening information—Marvin's commercials and loud sports jackets were indeed deceptive—when Ivy wended her way through the crowd, looking smart in a jump suit of pale blue silk belted with a slender band of rhinestones. Her aquamarine eyes took in Shay's outfit with approval. "Jeannie sent me to bid you welcome. She's in the kitchen, trying to pry an ice sculpture out of the freezer. Would you believe it's a perfect replica of *Venus de Milo?*"

"Now we know why the poor girl has no arms," Todd quipped, standing just behind Ivy.

Both Ivy and Shay groaned at the joke, and Ivy added a well-aimed elbow that splashed a few drops of champagne out of Todd's glass and onto his impeccable black jacket.

"Six months till the wedding and I'm already henpecked," he complained.

"I've been thinking about those condos," Mitch reflected distractedly. "From an ecological standpoint..."

"Business!" Ivy hissed, dragging Shay away by one arm. They came to a stop in front of a table spread with plates of wilted crab puffs, smoked oysters, crackers and cheeses.

Shay cast one look in Mitch's direction and saw that he was engrossed in his conversation with Todd. It hurt a little that he apparently hadn't even noticed that she was gone. She took a crab puff to console herself.

Ivy frowned pensively at the morsel. "Isn't that pathetic? You'd think a place as big as Skyler Beach would have one decent caterer, wouldn't you? Mrs. Reese had to have everything brought in from Seattle."

The crab puffs definitely showed the rigors of the journey, and it was a miracle that *Venus de Milo* had made it so far without melting into a puddle. Shay's dream of starting her own catering business surfaced and she pushed it resolutely back onto a mental shelf. She had a child to support and there was no way she could afford to take the financial risks such a venture would involve.

"You look fantastic!" Ivy whispered. "Is that blouse heavy?"

"It weighs a ton," Shay confided. Her eyes were following Mitch; she was memorizing every expression that crossed his face.

"Let's separate those two before they start drawing up plans or something," Ivy said lightly.

Shay wondered how long it would be before Todd balked at Ivy's gentle commandeering but made no comment. A buffet supper was served soon afterward, and she and Mitch sat alone in a corner of the beach house's enormous deck, listening to the chatter of the tide as they ate. Stars as bright as the sequins on Shay's blouse were popping out all over a black velvet sky and the summer breeze was warm.

When silences had fallen between herself and Eliott, Shay had always been uncomfortable, needing to riddle the space with words. With Mitch, there were no gaps to fill. It was all right to be quiet, to reflect and to dream.

Presently, a caterer's assistant came and collected their empty plates and glasses, but Mitch and Shay remained in that shadowy corner of the deck. When the Reeses' stereo system began to pipe soft music into the night, they moved together without speaking. They danced, and the proximity of Mitch's blatantly masculine body to Shay's softer one was an exquisite misery.

Shay saw his mouth descending to claim her own and instead of turning to avoid his kiss, she welcomed it. Unconsciously she braced herself for the crushing ardor Eliott had taught her to expect, but Mitch's kiss was gentle, tentative, almost questioning. She felt the tip of his tongue encircle her lips and a delicious tingling sensation spread into every part of her. His nearly inaudible groan rippled over her tongue and tickled the inner walls of her cheeks as she opened her mouth to him.

Gently, ever so gently, he explored her, his body pinning hers to the deck railing in a tender dominance that she welcomed, for rather than demanding submission, the gesture incited a passion so intense that Shay was terrified by it. Had it been feelings like these that had caused Rosamond to flit from one husband to another, dragging one very small and frightened daughter after her?

Shay turned her head, remembering the bewilderment and the despair. No one knew better than she did that the price of a grand passion could be a child's sense of security, and she wasn't going to let that happen to Hank.

"I'd like to go home," she managed to say.

Mitch only nodded, and when Shay dared risk a glance at his profile, turned now toward the dark sea, she saw no anger in the line of his jaw or the muscles in his neck.

They left minutes later, pausing only to make plausible excuses to Marvin and Jeannie Reese, and they had traveled nearly half an hour before Mitch broke the silence with a quiet, "I'm sorry, Shay."

Shay was miserable; she was still pulsing with the raw desire Mitch had aroused in her. Her breasts were weighted, as though bursting with some nectar only he could relieve them of, the nipples pulled into aching little buds, and a heavy throbbing in her abdomen signaled her body's preparation for a gratification that would be denied it. "I just—I guess I'm just not ready." Like hell you're not ready, she taunted herself.

"I wasn't going to make love to you with half of Skyler Beach just a wall away," Mitch pointed out reasonably. "Nor did I intend to fling you down in the sand, though now that I think about it, it doesn't sound like such a bad idea.''

Shay had forgotten all about the party while Mitch was kissing her anyway and the reminder of that stung her to fury. ''What exactly was your plan?'' she snapped.

''I was in no condition to plan anything, lady. We're talking primitive responses here.''

Shay lowered her head. She'd been trying to lay all the blame for what had nearly happened on Mitch and that was neither fair nor realistic. The only sensible thing to do now was change the subject. ''You said we would talk after the party. About why you were at Seaview this morning.''

''And we will. My place or yours?''

Did he think she was insane? Either place would be too private and yet a restaurant might be too public. ''Mitch, I want to know why you're interested in my mother's illness, and I want to know right now.''

''I never explore potentially emotional subjects in a moving vehicle.''

''Then stop this car!''

''Along a moonlit beach? Come on, Shay. Surely you know what's going to happen if I do that.''

Shay did know and she still wanted him to stop, which made her so mad that she turned in her seat and ignored him until they reached Skyler Beach. He drove toward her house, chivalrously giving her a choice between asking him in or spending a whole night in an agony of curiosity about his visit to Seaview. There would be agony aplenty without that.

''I'll make some coffee,'' Shay said stiffly.

He simply inclined his head, that brazen tenderness dancing in his eyes. Moments later he was seated at the table in Shay's small spotless kitchen, his gray jacket draped over the chair back. "What did Ivy tell you about me?"

Shay, filling the coffeepot with cold water, stiffened. "Not much. Come to think of it, I don't even know what you do for a living." It was humiliating, not knowing even that much about a man who had nearly made love to her on a sundeck.

"I'm a journalist."

Shay set the coffeepot aside, water and all, not even bothering to fill the basket with grounds. She fell into a chair of her own. "I don't understand."

"I think you do understand, Shay," he countered gently.

Shay felt tears gather in her eyes, stinging and hot. To hide them, she averted her face. "You plan to write about my mother, I suppose."

"Yes."

Swift, simmering anger made Shay meet his gaze. Damn, but it hurt to know that he hadn't taken her to the party just because he found her attractive and wanted her company! "I think you'd better leave."

Mitch sat easily in his chair, giving no indication whatsoever that he meant to do as Shay had asked. "I could have lied to you, you know. Won your confidence and then presented you with a fait accompli."

"I imagine you're very practiced at that, Mr. Prescott. Winning people's confidence, I mean, and then betraying them." She remembered the coffeepot and went back to measure in the grounds, which sprinkled the counter because she was shaking, put the lid on and plug the thing in. "Surely you don't write for one of those cheap supermarket scandal sheets—that would never pay you enough money to buy a house like yours.''

"I write books," he said, unruffled. "Under a pen name."

Shay leaned back against the counter's edge, the coffeepot chortling behind her, and folded her arms across her glitzy chest. "So my mother rates a real book, does she? Well, I'm sorry, Mr. Prescott, but there will be no book!"

"I'm afraid there will."

Shay went back to the table and sat down again. "I won't permit it! I'll sue!"

"You don't have to permit anything—unauthorized biographies are perfectly legal. Moreover, nothing would make my publisher happier than a lawsuit filed by Rosamond Dallas's daughter. The publicity would be well worth any settlement they, or I, might have to pay."

Shay felt the color drain from her face. What Mitch said made a dreadful sort of sense.

"I would have turned the project down cold, Shay," he went on, "except for one thing."

Shay sat up a little straighter. "What 'one thing' was that? Money?"

"I have plenty of money. Have you ever heard of Lucetta White?"

Lucetta White. Shay searched her memory and remembered the woman as the one person Rosamond had truly feared. Ms. White's books could be lethal to a career, every word as sharply honed as a razor's edge. "She ruined half a dozen of my mother's friends."

Mitch nodded. "Lucetta and I have the same agent. If I don't write this book, Shay, she will."

Shay felt sick at the prospect. "What assurance do I have that you'll be any kinder?"

"This. I'd like you to co-author the book. The by-line is yours, if you want it."

Thinking of other books written by the children of movie stars, Shay shook her head. "I couldn't."

"You couldn't help, or you couldn't claim the by-line?"

"I won't exploit my own mother," Shay said firmly. "Besides, I'm no writer."

"I'll handle that part of it. All I want is your input: memories, old scrapbooks, family pictures. In return, I'll pay you half of the advance and half of the royal-ties."

Shay swallowed hard. "You're talking about a considerable amount of money."

Again he nodded.

A kaleidoscope of possibilities fanned out and then merged in Shay's mind. She could provide for Hank's education, start her catering business....

"Would I have full control?"

Mitch was turning a teaspoon from end to end on the tabletop. "'Full control' is a very broad term. You can read all the material as we go along. I'll be as kind as I can, but I won't sugarcoat anything, and if I find a skeleton, I'll drag it out of the closet."

Shay's color flared, aching on her cheekbones and flowing in a hot rush down her neck. "That sounds like Lucetta White's method."

"Read a few of her books," Mitch answered briskly. "Lucetta invents her own skeletons, bone by grizzly bone."

The coffee was done, but Shay couldn't offer any, couldn't move from her chair. She rested her forehead in her palms. "I'll have to think about this."

She heard Mitch's chair scrape the linoleum floor as he stood up to go. "Fair enough. I'll call you in a few days."

Shay did not move until she had heard the front door open and close again. Then she went and locked it and watched through one of the picture windows as Mitch Prescott's Italian car pulled away.

Mitch waited for three days.

During those seventy-two endless hours, he hired a cook and a housekeeper and a gardener. He sent for the contents of his apartment in San Francisco, he sat at the microfilm machine in the public library, reading everything he could find concerning Rosamond Dallas, until the muscles in the small of his back threatened spasmodic rebellion.

On Tuesday morning, he drove to Reese Motors.

"Damn," Shay grumbled as she came out of the plush RV on the back lot.

Ivy tried very hard not to smile as she took in the yellow-and-black striped suit Shay was wearing. "I think you make a terrific bee," she said.

"Flattery," Shay answered bitterly, "will get you nowhere. Don't you dare laugh!"

Ivy put one hand over her mouth and the diamonds in her showy engagement ring sparkled in the sunshine. "Put the hat on. Here, let me help you."

Shay submitted to the hat, which was really more of a hood. It was black, with nodding antennae on top.

Richard Barrett approached with long strides. "The wings!" he thundered. "Where are the wings?"

"He thinks he's Cecil B. DeMille," Ivy whispered.

Shay, standing there in the hot sun, sweltering in her padded velveteen bee suit, wanted to slap him. "Wings?" she hissed.

"Of course," Richard replied with the kind of patience usually reserved for deaf dogs. "Bees do have wings, you know."

The wings were hunted down by Richard's curvaceous young assistant, who was taking this taste of show biz very seriously. She wore her sunglasses on top of her head and constantly consulted her clipboard.

"I don't need this job, you know," Shay muttered to no one in particular as she was shuffled onto an *X* chalked on the asphalt in front of an '82 Chrysler with air-conditioning.

"Do you remember your lines?" Richard's cretin assistant sang, blowing so that her fluffy auburn bangs danced in midair.

"Sure," Shay snapped. "To bee or not to bee, that is the question."

"Sheesh," the assistant marveled, not getting the joke.

"All right, Shay," Richard said, indicating one of two portable video cameras with a nod of his head. "We'll be filming from two angles, but I want you to look into this camera while you're delivering your line."

"Since when is 'bzzzz' a line?"

"Just do as I tell you, Shay." A muscle under Richard's right eye was jumping. Shay had never noticed that he had a twitch before.

"I'm ready," she conceded.

The cameras made an almost imperceptible whirring sound and a clapboard was snapped in her face.

"Take One!" Richard cried importantly.

"Bzzzzzz," said Shay, dancing around the hood of the Chrysler as though to pollinate it. "Come to Reese Motors, in Skyler Beach, 6832 Discount Way! You can't afford to miss a honey of a deal like this!" She moved on to a '78 Pinto. So far, so good. "Take this little model right here, only nineteen-ninety—nineteen-ninety—"

Shay's voice froze in her throat and her concentration fled. Mitch Prescott was standing beside Ivy, looking stunned.

"Cut!" Richard bellowed.

Shay swallowed, felt relieved as she watched Mitch turn and walk resolutely away. Were his shoulders shaking just a little beneath that pristine white shirt of his?

"I'm sorry," she said to Richard, who looked apoplectic. It seemed to Shay that he took commercials a mite too seriously.

"Take Two," Richard groaned. "God, why do I work with amateurs? Somebody tell me why!"

He wouldn't have dared to talk to Marvin that way, Shay thought. And why had she apologized, anyway? Nobody got a commercial right on the first take, did they?

Shay waited for the camera to click into action and then started over, offering the folks in Skyler Beach a bunny of a deal.

"That's Easter!" Richard screamed, frustrated beyond all good sense.

"Don't get your stinger in a wringer!" the bee screamed back and every salesman on the lot roared with laughter.

On the third take the spot was flawless. Shay scowled at Richard and stomped into the RV with Ivy right behind her. The younger woman kept biting back giggles as she helped with the cumbersome costume.

When Shay was back in her white slacks and golden, imitation-silk blouse, her hair brushed and her make-up back to normal, she left the RV with her chin held high. The salesmen formed a double line, a sort of good-natured gauntlet, and applauded and cheered as she passed.

Shay executed a couple of regal bows, but her cheeks were throbbing with embarrassment by the time she closed her office door behind her and sank against it. It was bad enough that half of Washington state would see that stupid commercial. Why had Mitch had to see it, too?

Chapter Five

The very fact of Marvin's absence seemed to generate problems and Shay was grateful for the distraction. Dealing with the complaints and questions of customers kept her from thinking about the three commercials yet to be filmed and the very enticing dangers of working closely with Mitch Prescott.

At five minutes to five, Ivy waltzed into Shay's office with a mischievous light in her eyes and a florist's bouquet in her hands. "For you," she said simply, setting the arrangement of pink daisies interspersed with baby's breath and white carnations square on top of Shay's paperwork.

At the sight and scent of the flowers, Shay felt a peculiar shakiness in the pit of her stomach. Reason said the lovely blossoms had been sent by the salesmen downstairs or perhaps the Reeses. Instinct said something very different.

Her hands trembling just slightly—she couldn't remember the last time anyone had sent her flowers—Shay reached out for the envelope containing the card. Instinct prevailed. "If you're free tonight, let's discuss the book over dinner at my place. Strictly business, I promise. R.S.V.P. Mitch."

Strictly business, he said. Shay remembered Mitch's kiss and the sweet, hard pressure of his body against her own on the Reeses' darkened deck the night of the party and wondered who the hell he thought he was kidding. She felt a certain annoyance, a tender dreading, but mingled with these emotions was a sensation of heady relief. With a sigh, Shay admitted to herself that she would have been very disappointed if the flowers had come from anyone else on the face of the earth.

"Mitch?" Ivy asked, the impish light still dancing in her eyes.

Shay grinned. "How very redundant of you to ask. You knew."

"I did not!" Ivy swore with conviction and just a hint of righteous indignation. "I just guessed, that's all."

Shay's weariness dropped away and she moved the vase of flowers to clear the paperwork from her desk. She sensed all the eager questions Ivy wanted to ask and enjoyed withholding the answers. "Well," she said with an exaggerated sigh, picking up her purse and the flowers and starting toward the door, "I'll see you tomorrow. Have a good evening."

Ivy was right on her heels. "Oh, no you don't, Shay Kendall! Did my brother ask you out or what? Why did he send you flowers? What did the card *say*, exactly?"

Smiling to herself, Shay walked rapidly toward the stairs. To spare her friend a night of agonizing curiosity, she tossed back an off-handed "He wants to start work on the book about Rosamond. Good night, Ivy."

"What book?" Ivy cried desperately, hurrying to keep up with Shay as she went down the stairs and across the polished floor of the main display room. "You don't mean—you're not actually—you said you'd never—"

Fortunately, Todd was waiting for Ivy outside, or she might have followed Shay all the way to her car, battering her with questions and fractured sentences.

Ivy looked so pained as her fiancé ushered her into the passenger seat of his car that Shay called out a merciful, "I promise I'll explain tomorrow," as she got behind the wheel of her own car.

Shay did not drive toward home; Hank wouldn't be there and she needed some time to prepare herself for the strange quiet that would greet her when she unlocked her front door. She decided to pay her mother a visit.

More than once during the short drive to Seaview Convalescent Home, Shay glanced toward the flowers so carefully placed on the passenger seat and wondered if it wouldn't be safer, from an emotional standpoint anyway, to forget Mitch Prescott and this collaboration business altogether and take her chances with Lucetta White. Granted, the woman was a literary viper, but Ms. White couldn't hurt Rosamond, could she? No one could hurt Rosamond.

Shay bit her lower lip as she turned into the spacious asphalt parking lot behind the convalescent home. Rosamond was safe, but what about Hank? What about Riley and Garrett? What about herself?

Stopping the car and turning off the ignition, Shay rested her forehead on the steering wheel and drew a deep breath. Each life, she reflected, feeling bruised and cornered, touches other lives. If Miss White chose to, she could drag up all sorts of hurtful things, such as Eliott's theft all those years before, and his desertion. Shay had long since come to terms with Eliott's actions, but how could Hank, a six-year-old, be expected to understand and cope?

Shay drew another deep breath and sat up very straight. Except for his personal word, she had no assurances that Mitch Prescott would be any fairer or any kinder in his handling of the Rosamond Dallas story, but he did seem the lesser of two evils, even considering the unnerving effect he had on Shay's emotions. The book would be written, one way or the other, and there was no going back.

She got out of the car, crossed the parking lot and entered the convalescent home resolutely. Shay was not looking forward to another one-sided visit with her mother and the guilt inspired by that fact made her spirits sag. What was she supposed to say to the woman? "Hello, Mother, today I dressed up as a bee?" Or maybe she could announce, "Guess what? I've met a man and he wants to tell all your most intimate secrets to the world and I'm going to help him and for all that, Mother, I do believe he could seduce me without half trying!"

As Shay hurried through the rear entrance to the building and down the immaculate hallway toward her mother's room, the inner dialogue gained momentum. *I'm afraid, Mother. I'm afraid. I'm starting to care about Mitch Prescott and that's going to make everything that much more difficult, don't you see? We'll make love and that will change me for always but it will just be another affair to him. I don't think I could bear that, Mother.*

Overcome, Shay stopped and rested one shoulder against the wall beside Rosamond's door, her head lowered. The fantasy was futile: Rosamond couldn't advise her, probably wouldn't bother even if she were well. That was reality.

A cold, quiet anger sustained Shay, made her square her shoulders and lift her chin. She walked into her mother's room, crossed to her chair, bent to bestow the customary forehead kiss. Then, because her own reality was that she loved her mother, whether that love had ever been returned or not, Shay sat down facing Rosamond and told her about being a bee in a car-lot commercial, about a bouquet of pink daisies, about a man with brash brown eyes and a smile that made grooves in his cheeks.

After half an hour, when Rosamond's dinner was brought in, Shay slipped out. She hesitated only a moment before the pay phone in the hallway, then rummaged through her purse for a quarter. Mitch answered on the second ring.

"Thank you for the flowers," Shay said lamely. She'd planned a crisper approach, but at the sound of his voice, the words had evaporated from her mind in a shimmering fog.

His responding chuckle was a low, tender sound, rich with the innate masculinity he exuded so effortlessly. "You're welcome. Now, what about dinner and the book?"

Shay, whose job and personal responsibilities had always forced her to be strong, suddenly ached with shyness. "Strictly business?" she croaked out.

Mitch's silence was somehow endearing, as though he had reached out to caress her cheek or smooth her hair back from her face, but it was also brief. "Until we both decide otherwise, princess," he said softly. "You're not walking into any heavy scenes, so relax. You're safe with me."

Tears filled Shay's eyes, coming-home tears, in-out-of-the-rain tears. She would be safe with Mitch, and that was a new experience for Shay, one she had never had with Rosamond or Eliott. "Thanks," she managed to say.

"No problem," came the velvety yet gruff reply. "Remember, though, I'm not promising that I won't tease you about this morning."

Shay found herself laughing, a moist sound making its way through receding tears. "If you think the bee debacle was bad, wait until you hear about my next epic."

"The suspense is killing me," Mitch replied with good-natured briskness, but then his voice was soft again, at once vulnerable and profoundly reassuring. "It looks as though it might rain. Drive carefully, Shay."

"What time do you want me?"

Mitch laughed. "You name a time, baby, and I want you."

"Let me rephrase that," retorted Shay, smiling. "What time is dinner?"

"Now. Whenever." He paused, sighed in exasperation. "Shay, just get over here, before I go crazy."

"Can you stay sane for half an hour? I want to change clothes."

She could almost see his eyebrows arch. "Wear the bee suit," he answered. "It really turns me on."

Shaking her head, Shay said goodbye and hung up. Her step was light as she hurried down into the hallway and outside to her car. The sky had clouded over, just as Mitch had said, and there was a muggy, prestorm heaviness in the summer air. Shay blamed her sense of sweet foreboding on the weather.

At home, she quickly showered, put on trim gray slacks and a lightweight sweater to match, reapplied her makeup and gave her damp hair a vigorous brushing. It was a glistening mane of softness, tumbling sensuously to her shoulders and she decided that the look was entirely too come-hither. With a few brisk motions, she wound it into a chignon and then stood back from the bathroom mirror a little way to assess herself. Yes, indeed, she looked like the no-nonsense type all right. "Strictly business," she reminded her image aloud, before turning away.

Since his new housekeeper, Mrs. Carraway, had left for the day, Mitch answered the door himself. He knew the visitor would be Shay, and yet he felt surprised at the sight of her, not only surprised, but jarred.

She was wearing gray slacks and a V-necked sweater to match. Her makeup was carefully understated and her hair was done up, instead of falling gracefully around her shoulders as it usually did, and Mitch suppressed a smile. Obviously she had made every effort to look prim, but the effect was exactly the opposite: she had achieved a sexy vulnerability that made him want her all the more.

For several moments, Mitch just stood there, staring at her like a fool. The cymballike clap of thunder roused him, however, and he remembered his manners and moved back from the doorway. "Come in."

Shay stepped into the house with a timid sort of bra-
vado that touched Mitch deeply. Were her memories of
the place sad ones, or were they happy? He wanted to
know that and so much more, but getting close to this
woman was a process that required a delicate touch; she
was like some wild, beautiful, rarely seen creature of the
forests, ready to flee at the slightest threat.

"Your things haven't arrived," she said, her eyes
sweeping the massive empty foyer swiftly, as though in
an effort not to see too much.

Gently, Mitch took her elbow in his hand, still fearing that she would bolt like a unicorn sensing a trap.
"Actually," he answered in a tone he hoped sounded
casual, "some of them have. All the most impractical
things, anyway: pots and pans but no plates, sheets and
pillows but no bed..."

He instantly regretted mentioning the bed.

Shay only smiled. She was relaxing, if only slightly.

They ate in the library, picnic-style, before a snapping, summer-storm fire, their paper plates balanced on
their laps, their wine contained in supermarket glasses.
For all that, there was an ambiance of elegance to the
scenario, and Mitch knew that it emanated from the
woman who sat facing him. What a mystery she was,
what a tangle of vulnerability and strength, softness and
fire, humor and tragedy.

Mitch felt his own veneer of sophistication, something he had long considered immutable, dissolving
away. His reactions to that were ambivalent, of course;
he was a man who controlled situations—at times his
life had depended on that control—but now, in the
presence of this woman, he was strangely powerless.
The surprising thing was that he was comfortable with
that.

When the meal was over he disposed of the plates and the plastic wineglasses and returned to the library to find Shay standing in the center of the room, studying every bookcase, every stone in the fireplace.

"Were you happy here?" he asked, without intending to speak at all.

She started and then turned slowly to face him. "Yes," she said.

The ache in Shay's wide hazel eyes came to settle somewhere in the middle of Mitch's chest. "Feel free to explore," he said after a rather long silence.

A quiet joy displaced the pain in Shay's face and Mitch was relieved. "But we were going to work," she offered halfheartedly. "I brought the photo albums you wanted. They're in the car and—"

Mitch spoke with the abruptness typical of nervous people. "I'll get them while you look around. Maybe you can give me a few decorating ideas. Right now, this place has all the cozy warmth of an abandoned coal mine."

She looked grateful and just a little suspicious. "Well..."

Mitch pretended that the matter had been settled and left the house. Her car was parked in the driveway, only a few strides from the front door, and the box containing Rosamond Dallas's memorabilia was sitting in plain sight on the seat. He took his time carrying the stuff inside, setting it on the library floor, sorting through it. Instinctively he knew that Shay needed time to wander from room to room, settling memories.

The room that had been Shay's was empty, of course. The built-in bookshelves were bare and dusty, the French provincial furniture and frilly bedclothes had been removed, along with the host of stuffed animals and the antique carousel horse, a gift from Riley Thompson, that had once stood just to the left of the cushioned windowseat. The nostalgia Shay had braced herself for did not come, however; this had been the room of a child and she felt no desire to go backward in time.

She wandered across the wide hallway and into the suite that had been Rosamond's, in a strange, quiet mood. The terrace doors were open to the rising rain-and-sea misted wind and Shay crossed the barren room to close them. She smiled as she stepped over the tangled sleeping bag that had been spread out on the floor, and a certain scrumptious tension gripped her as she imagined Mitch lying there.

He was downstairs, waiting for her, but Shay could not bring herself to hurry. She reached down and took a pillow from the floor and held it to her face. Its scent was Mitch's scent, a mingling of sun-dried clothing and something else that was indefinably his own.

Shay knelt on the sleeping bag, still holding the pillow close and, unreasonably, inexplicably, tears filled her eyes. She couldn't think why, because she didn't feel sad and she didn't feel happy, either. She felt only a need to be held.

It was as though she had called out—in the future Shay would wonder many times whether or not she had—because Mitch suddenly appeared in the double doorway of the suite. "Are you all right?" he asked, and Shay knew that he was keeping his distance, honoring his promise that she would be safe with him.

And she didn't want to be safe. "No," she answered. "Actually, no."

Mitch crossed the room then, knelt before her, removed the pillow from her grip and cupped her face in his strong hands, his thumbs moving to dry away her tears.

Shay was reminded of that other time when he'd held her, before the party, when she had dissolved over a bucket of take-out chicken at the backyard picnic table. "I'm not usually such a c-crybaby," she stammered out. "You must think—"

"I think you're beautiful," he said. It was what any healthy man on the verge of a seduction would say, Shay supposed, but coming from Mitch Prescott it sounded sincere. A tremulous, electric need was surging through her, starting where his hands touched her face so gently, settling into sweet chaos in her breasts and deep within her middle. She couldn't think.

"Hold me," she said.

Mitch held her and she knew that the line had been irrevocably crossed. He kissed her, just a tentative, nibbling kiss, and the turmoil within her grew fierce. This facet of Shay's womanhood, denied for six years and largely unfulfilled before that, was now beyond the realm of good judgment: it was a thing of instinct.

But Mitch drew back, his hands on Shay's shoulders now, his expression somber in the shadowy half light of that enormous, empty room. "Remember what I said earlier, Shay? About both of us being ready?"

Shay couldn't speak; her throat was twisted into a raw knot. She managed to nod.

The low timbre of Mitch's voice resounded with misgivings. "I don't want this to be something you regret later, Shay, something that drives a wedge between us. Being close to you is too important to me."

Shay swallowed hard and was able to get out a soft, broken "I need you."

"I know," came the unhurried answer, "and I feel the same way. But for you this house is full of ghosts, Shay. What you need from me may be something entirely different than what I need from you." As if to test his theory, he held her, his hands strong on her back, comforting her but making no demands.

She rested her forehead against his shoulder, breathing deeply, trying to get control of herself. "You're wrong," she said after a long, careful silence. "I'm not Rosamond Dallas's little girl, haunting this house. I'm—I'm a woman, Mitch."

He chuckled, his breath moving warm in her hair, his hands still kneading the tautness of her back. "You are definitely a woman," he agreed. "No problems there."

Shay moved her hands, sliding them boldly beneath his sweater so that she could caress his chest, and her touch brought an involuntary groan from him, along with a muttered swearword.

Shay laughed and fell to the down-filled softness of the sleeping bag, and Mitch descended with her, one of his hands coming to rest on her thigh with a reluctant buoyancy that made it bounce away and then return again, albeit unwillingly.

"We're both going to regret this," he grumbled, but his hand was beneath her sweater now, caressing the inward curve of her waist.

That remark made sense to Shay, but she was beyond caring. There was only the needing now. "It was inevitable...."

Mitch was kissing the pulsing length of her neck, the outline of her jaw. "That it was," he agreed, and then his mouth reached hers, claiming it gently.

Shay shuddered with delicious sensations as his hand roamed up her rib cage to claim one lace-covered breast. With a practiced motion that would have been disturbing if it hadn't felt so wonderful; he displaced her bra and took her full into his hand, stroking the nipple with the side of his thumb.

She felt a shudder to answer her own move through his body as he stretched out beside her, the kiss unbroken. A primitive, silent whimpering pounded through Shay and she was glad that Mitch couldn't hear it. She wriggled to lie beneath him, needing the weight and pressure of him as much as she needed the ultimate possession they were moving toward.

He groaned at this and ended the kiss, but only to slide Shay's sweater upward, baring her inch by inch. She felt the garment pass away, soon followed by the skimpy bra beneath. She wondered why she'd worn that bra, when she'd dressed to fend off just what was happening now. Or had she dressed to invite it?

"Oh," she said, gasping the word, as Mitch's mouth closed boldly around her nipple and drove all coherent thought from her mind. His hand found the junction of her thighs, still covered by her slacks and panties, and the skilled motions of his fingers caused her hips to leap in frenzied greeting. Just when she would have begged for closer contact, he gave it, deftly undoing the button and zipper of her slacks, sliding them away into the nothingness that had taken her sweater and all her inhibitions. Her panties and sandals were soon gone, too.

"God in heaven," Mitch muttered as he drew back to look at her. He stripped off his own clothes and returned to her unwillingly, as though flung to her by forces he could not resist.

Mitch's hands caressed and stroked every part of her, until she was writhing in a tender delirium, searching him out with her fingers and her mouth, with every part of her. Finally he sat back on his muscled haunches and lifted Shay to sit astraddle of him, and she cried out as they became one in a single, leisurely stroke.

Even at the beginning, the pleasure was so great as to be nearly unbearable to Shay; she flung her head back and forth in response to the glorious ache that became greater with every motion of their joined bodies, and her hair fell from its pins and flew about her face and shoulders in a wild flurry of femininity.

All that was womanly in Shay called out to all that was masculine in Mitch and they moved as one to lie prone on the tangled sleeping bag, their bodies quickening in the most primal, most instinctive of quests. And then there was no man and there was no woman, for in the blinding explosion of satisfaction that gripped them and wrung a single shout of triumph from them both, they were one entity.

Afterward, as Shay lay trembling and dazed upon that sleeping bag, she tried to brace herself for the inevitable remorse. Incredibly she felt only brazen contentment. It was fortunate, in her view, that she didn't have the strength to talk.

Apparently, Mitch didn't either. He was lying with one leg thrust across hers, his chest moving in breaths so deep that they must have been carrying air all the way to his toes, his face buried in the warm curve where Shay's neck met her shoulder.

Long minutes had passed before he withdrew from her and crossed the room to take a robe from the closet and pull it on. The wrenching motions of his arms were angry, and the glorious inertia that had possessed Shay until that moment fled instantly.

Mitch left the room without speaking and Shay was too proud to call him back. She sat upright on the sleeping bag and covered herself with his shirt, chilled now that the contact had been broken not only physically, but emotionally. She waited in a small hell of confusion and shame, willing herself to put on her clothes and leave but unable to do so.

Finally, Mitch returned. He flipped on the lights, revealing the starkness of the room, the scattering of Shay's clothes and his own, the reality of the situation. Shay closed her eyes and let her forehead fall to her upraised knees.

He nudged her shoulder with something cold and she looked up to see that he was offering a glass of chilled wine. Blushing, Shay took it in both hands, but she could not meet his eyes.

"You're angry," she said miserably.

"Shocked would be a more appropriate word," he answered, sitting down nearby and clinking his own glass against hers.

Now, Shay's eyes darted to his face. She was stung to an anger that made her forget the one she had sensed in Mitch. "Shocked? You? The adventurer, the sophisticate?"

His expression had softened; in his eyes Shay saw some lingering annoyance, but this was overshadowed by a certain perplexity. "I wasn't casting aspersions on your moral character, Shay, so settle down."

"Then what were you doing?"

He only smiled at the snap in her voice, setting his wineglass aside with a slow, lazy motion of one hand. "From the moment I met you, you've been trying to keep me at a distance. You might as well have worn a sign saying Look, but Don't Touch. Yet tonight, you—''

She couldn't bear for him to say that she'd seduced him, though it was true, in a manner of speaking. "I'm a woman of the eighties!" she broke in, shrugging nonchalantly and lifting her wineglass in an insolent salute, though in truth she felt like sliding down inside the sleeping bag and hiding there.

"Yes," Mitch replied wryly. "The eighteen-eighties."

"I resent that!"

He took her wineglass and set it aside. "Strange. That's one of the most interesting things about you, you know. Despite what we just did, you're an innocent."

"Is that bad or good?"

He took the shirt she'd been clutching and flung it away, giving her bare breasts a wicked assessment with those quick, bold eyes of his. "I haven't decided yet," he said, and then they made love again, this time in the light.

Chapter Six

The box containing what remained of the Rosamond Dallas legend was a silent reprimand to Mitch. He rolled his head and worked the taut muscles in his neck with one hand. *You'll be safe with me,* he'd told Shay. No heavy scenes, he'd said.

He heard that ridiculous old car of hers grind to a start in the driveway and swore. She'd come there to have dinner and to work and instead she was making a getaway in the gray light of a drizzling dawn, afraid of encountering his housekeeper.

Mitch shook his aching head and swore again, but then a slow, weary smile broke over his face. He regretted buying the house and he regretted ever mentioning Rosamond Dallas to his agent, but he couldn't regret Shay. For better or for worse, she was the answer to all his questions.

He walked to the middle of the library floor, knelt on the carpet and began going through the photographs, diaries and clippings that made up Rosamond Dallas's life.

At home Shay took a hot, hasty shower and dressed for work. She kept waiting for the guilt, the remorse, the regret, but there were no signs of any such emotion. Her body still vibrated, like a fine instrument expertly played, and her mind, for the first time in years, was quiet.

While she brushed her hair and applied her makeup with more care than usual, Shay remembered the nights with Eliott and wondered what she'd seen in him.

She paused, lip pencil in midair, and gazed directly into the mirror. "Hold it, lady," she warned her reflection out loud. "One night on a man's sleeping bag does not constitute a pledge of eternal devotion, you know. Don't forget that you threw yourself at him like a—like a brazen hussy!" Shay frowned hard, for emphasis, but even those sage words, borrowed in part from one of her mother's early movies, could not dampen her soaring spirits. She was in love with Mitch Prescott, really in love, for the first time in her life, and for the moment, that was enough.

Of course, it made no sense to be so happy—there was every chance that she'd just made a mistake of epic proportions—but Shay didn't let that bother her either. Mitch's feelings, whatever they might be, were his own problem.

She drove to Reese Motors and soared into her office, only to find Ivy waiting in ambush. Even though the phones were ringing and Richard's camera crew was crowded into the reception room, Ms. Prescott sat quietly on Shay's couch, her legs crossed, her hands folded in her lap.

Shay smiled and shook her head. Love was marvelous. Richard's crew was proof positive that she was going to have to film another commercial that very day and here was Ivy, waiting to grill her about the evening with Mitch, and she still felt wonderful. "I hate to pull rank, Ivy," she said brightly, "but get out there and take care of business. Now."

Ivy looked hurt but nonetheless determined as she stood up and smoothed the skirt of her blue cotton dress. "At least promise to have lunch with me," she said with dignity. "You did say that you'd tell me all about everything, you know."

Shay thought about "everything" and blushed. There was no way she was going to tell everything. "We may not have time for lunch today, Ivy. There's another commercial scheduled, isn't there? And by the way that phone is jumping around on the desk, I'd say it's going to be a crazy day."

Ivy was sulking and just reaching for the doorknob when the door itself suddenly sprang open, the chasm filled by an earnest and somewhat testy Richard. "I know we planned to wait a week before we filmed the second spot, but something has come up and—"

Shay smiled placidly, knowing that the advertising executive had been prepared for a battle. "Come in, Richard," she said in a sweet voice. "Don't bother to knock."

Richard looked sheepish and somewhat baffled. He ran one hand through his already mussed hair and stared at Shay in speechless bewilderment.

She laughed. "Which one are we doing today?" she prompted lightly as Ivy dashed out and began answering the calls that were lighting up all the buttons on the telephone.

"The one you hated."

Shay was still unruffled. "That figures. When are they airing yesterday's artistic triumph?"

"Next week," Richard answered distractedly, glancing at his watch and frowning as though it had somehow displeased him. "Do you want the makeup done here, or down on the lot, in the RV?"

"I don't want it done at all, but I know wishful thinking when I see it. I'll be on down there in five or ten minutes."

Shay's intercom buzzed and she picked up the telephone receiver. "Yes, Ivy?"

"Hank's on line two," the secretary said pleasantly, her ire at being put off having faded away.

Delighted, Shay punched the second button on her telephone. "Hi, tiger!" she cried. "How are you?"

The sound of Hank's voice was the reward, Shay supposed, for some long-forgotten good deed. "I'm great, Mom! We're at this lake in Oregon and we caught two fish already!"

"That's fantastic!" Shay ignored Richard Barrett's alternating glares of impatience and consultations with his watch and turned to the windows. The sky was gray and drops of rain were bouncing off the cars in the rear lot. It was strange, she reflected fancifully, that she hadn't noticed the weather on her way to work. "Is it raining there?"

The conversation with her son was sweetly mundane and when it ended, five minutes later, Shay stoically followed Richard through the outer office and down the stairs. Due to the rain, the RV had been parked close to one of the rear entrances and the showroom itself would be the set.

Inside the roomy motor home, Shay was helped into a neck-to-toe bodysuit with metallic bolts of thunder stitched to it, and glittery cartoon superheroine make-up was applied to her face. As gooey styling mousse was poured into her hair, she tried to be philosophical. This was the silliest commercial of the lot, but it was also the easiest. She had only to say one line, and the remainder of the spot would show used cars with prices painted on their windshields.

"I bet you hate having your friends see you like this," commiserated Richard's assistant, she of the fluffy bangs and ever-present clipboard, as she pulled Shay's mousse-saturated tresses into points that stuck straight out, all over her head.

Shay only rolled her eyes, telling herself that the girl was young.

"I'd die," insisted the little helper.

"If you keep working for Richard," Shay replied, "your life will probably be short."

"Huh?"

"Here but for the grace of God go you, my dear."

"I still don't get it."

"Never mind," Shay said with a sigh. The mousse was drying and her scalp itched. The bodysuit was riding up in all the wrong places. She told herself that that was why she suddenly felt so uncharitable.

The door of the RV squeaked open and made the hollow sound typical of all motor homes when it closed behind Richard. He looked at Shay as though he'd just beaten her at some game and his mouth twitched. "I," he said with quiet pomposity, "am a genius."

"Don't press your luck, Richard," Shay snarled. Her body was no longer vibrating, and there was a headache unfolding behind her right temple.

"I said I'd die if I had to dress like that and she said my life might be short if I went on working for you," broke in the assistant in a breathless babble. "What'd she mean by that, Richard? She won't tell me what she meant!"

"Wait outside, Chrissie," Richard said, all but patting the girl on the head.

Reluctantly, Chrissie obeyed.

"Does your wife know about her?" Shay asked, just to be mean.

Richard cleared his throat and pressed at his hopelessly old-fashioned glasses with one index finger. Despite this display of nervousness, he was not an easy opponent. "You have an audience outside," he said. "Why, darlin', your fame is spreadin' like wildfire!"

Shay stood up with a sigh. "That was the worst imitation of J.R. Ewing I've ever heard," she snapped.

Richard only shrugged, and when they entered the showroom moments later, Shay was even more annoyed to find that she did indeed have an audience. All of the salesmen were there, along with their wives and even a few children. It was the presence of the children that kept Shay from showing them that she was Rosamond Dallas's daughter by making a scene.

"Stand right there on your *X*, darlin'," Richard drawled in the same bad Texas accent. "This'll be over before you can say—"

"Oh, shut up!" Shay grumbled, taking her mark.

The lights were blaring in her face. She drew a deep breath and tried to be professional, which wasn't easy in a thunderbolt bodysuit and outrageous makeup.

Mentally she went over her line. Oh, to do this in one take and have it behind her!

The clapboard snapped in her face and Shay smiled broadly, trying not to think of how her hair was standing out from her head in mousse-crusted points. She knew she looked as though she had just stuck her finger into a light socket, and that, of course, was the whole idea. "Come out and see for yourselves, folks," she crowed winningly. "Our prices here at Reese Motors, 6832 Discount Way, are so low that they'll shock you!"

It was a wrap! Shay wanted to jump up into the air, Mickey Rooney-style, and click her heels together.

"Do it again," Richard said with exaggerated patience.

Shay couldn't have been more surprised if he'd doused her in cold water. "What?" she demanded. "Richard, that take was perfect!"

"It wasn't anything of the sort. I want more emphasis on the word 'shock.'"

He was repaying her for the barbs they'd exchanged inside the RV and that knowledge infuriated Shay. "I think this gunk in my hair makes that point on its own, don't you?"

"No," Richard responded flatly.

He made her go through the scene half a dozen times before he would admit to any sort of satisfaction with it, and that, when he gave it, was grudging.

Shay muttered as she stomped back into the RV and slammed the door behind her. Refusing help from the vacuous Chrissie, she slathered cleansing cream onto her face and carefully wiped away the glittery makeup. After that, she squeezed into the vehicle's miniature bathroom and took a tepid shower, muttering through shampoo after shampoo. A bathrobe that probably belonged to Marvin was hanging on the hook inside the door, and Shay helped herself to it.

When she left the bathroom she was startled to find Mitch Prescott sitting at the RV's tiny table, his hair moussed into an elongated crew cut rising a good four inches above his head. "May I say," he told her blandly, "that I was shocked by your behavior this morning?"

The utter ridiculousness of the moment dissolved Shay's foul mood, and she began to laugh. "You're crazy!"

Mitch caught her hand and pulled her onto his lap. "About you," he said, on cue.

Shay knew that she shouldn't be sitting on this man's lap in an oversized bathrobe with all of Reese Motors's employees gathered outside, but she was powerless to move away. She looked at Mitch's hair and into his laughing brown eyes and she thought, *I love you. God help me, I love you.*

Mischievously he opened the front of her robe, revealing her breasts, and she could not lift a hand to stop him. "It's a good thing you washed that stuff out of your hair," he mumbled distractedly, and she could feel his breath on her right breast, feel the nipple tensing for the touch of his tongue. It came soon enough, and Shay gasped, the sensation was so wickedly delicious.

"Why?" she groaned.

"Because we might have mated and produced a punk rocker," he answered sleepily, still busy with her breast.

Using laughter and the last bit of her willpower, Shay thrust herself off Mitch's lap and out of his reach. Watching her, he helped himself to a hairbrush left behind by Chrissie and returned his hair to some semblance of normalcy. Shay wanted to use that time to dress and escape, but she couldn't seem to work up the momentum.

When the maestro held out his hands, she moved into them, moaning softly as she stood before Mitch, shivering as she felt the robe open. The intermezzo was a sweet one, brief and soaring, underscored by Shay's own soft cries of pleasure as she was taught a new tune, note by glorious note.

Minutes later, fully dressed, she left the RV with her head held high and her body humming. The vibrations carried her through the rest of the day.

If the night before had been given over to dalliance, that one was all business. The rest of Mitch's furniture had arrived and he and Shay sat on a sinfully soft burgundy sofa in his library, facing each other instead of the crackling fire, half-buried in scrapbooks and old photographs.

As she explained what she knew of her mother's life, Shay found herself thrust from one emotional extreme to another, from laughter to tears, from love to anger. Mitch only listened, making no move to touch her.

"Sometimes," Shay confided pensively as the long evening drew toward a close, "I think she was the most selfish person on earth. Riley loved her so much, and yet..."

The small cassette recorder between them hummed and whirred. "Yes?" prompted Mitch.

"I think that was the very reason that Rosamond began to lose interest in him. Finally she seemed to feel nothing but contempt. But Riley was such a good man, so decent and solid—it just doesn't make sense!"

"Since when are legendary movie stars expected to make sense?"

Shay shrugged and then yawned. "Rosamond certainly didn't."

"She must have made you angry," Mitch remarked, snapping off the recorder with a motion of his hand.

The words jarred Shay out of her sleepy stupor. Suddenly she didn't want to talk about Rosamond anymore, and she didn't want to talk about herself. "I'd better be going," she said, moving to rise off the sofa.

Mitch stopped her by taking her arm in a gentle grasp. "She did make you angry, didn't she?" he persisted quietly.

"No."

"You're lying."

Shay bounded off the couch and this time there was no stopping her. "Who do you think you are?" she snapped. "Sigmund Freud?"

Mitch sat back in that cushy sofa, damn him, and cupped his hands behind his head, not saying so much as a word. Shay was reminded of the scandalous way he'd loved her in the RV earlier and she sat down in a nearby chair, her knees weak.

"Everybody has hang-ups about their mother," she sputtered when the silence grew too long and too damning. She glared at Mitch, remembering all that Ivy had told her over the past few years. "Or their stepmother."

Mitch sighed and stared up at the ceiling, still maintaining his attitude of relaxed certainty. "The difference is, my dear, that I can talk about my stepmother. She and I don't get along because she was my father's mistress before he and my mother were divorced. In effect, you could say that she took him away from us."

"My God," Shay whispered, feeling sympathy even though there was nothing in Mitch's voice or manner that asked for it.

"It was traumatic at the time," Mitch said evenly. "But Dad was a good father to me and, eventually, my mother remarried. She's disgustingly happy."

"But Ivy's mother—"

"Elizabeth does the best she can. She loved my father."

Shay was silent.

"Your turn," Mitch prompted.

She stared into the snapping fire for a while, drifting back to another night. "Rosamond was her own greatest fan," she said. "And yet she could humiliate herself so easily. I remember one of her lovers—a tennis bum—he was good-looking but if you tapped on his forehead, nobody would answer the door."

Mitch chuckled. "Go on."

"He was part of the reason that Mother got bored with Riley, I guess. After Riley and Garrett were gone, he decided that it was time to get back on the old circuit. He was going to walk out and I'll never forget—I'll never forget the way Mother acted. He was trying to get into his car and she was on her knees in the driveway, with her arms wrapped around his legs, begging him to stay." Shay turned shadowed, hurting eyes to Mitch's face. "It was awful."

"You saw that?" Mitch must have tried, but he failed to keep the annoyance out of his voice.

"I've seen a lot worse," she answered.

"Stay with me," he said, clearing away aging memorabilia to make a space beside him on the sofa.

Shay couldn't leave, but she suddenly felt too broken and vulnerable to stay. "I don't want—"

"I know," he said, standing up and extending one hand to her. After a moment or so, she rose and took the offered hand and Mitch led her gently up the stairs and into his bedroom.

Furnished now with a massive waterbed, chairs and bureaus and a freestanding chess table set up for play, the room didn't seem so vast.

Deftly, as though he did such things as a part of his daily routine, Mitch undressed Shay and then buttoned her into one of his pajama tops, a royal blue silk affair with piping and a monogram on the pocket.

"You do not strike me as a man who wears pajamas," she said, aware of the inanity of her remark but too shaky to say anything heavier.

"A Christmas present from Ivy," he explained, disappearing into the adjoining bathroom. A moment later Shay heard the shower running.

"Why am I staying here?" she asked the cosmos, holding her arms out from her sides.

When the cosmos didn't answer, she followed Mitch into the steamy chamber and helped herself to one of the new toothbrushes she found in the cabinet drawer. As she brushed, she fumed. Six toothbrushes, still in their boxes. The man expected to entertain a harem!

Behind the beautifully etched door of the double shower, Mitch sang at the top of his lungs. Shay glared at her reflection in the steamy mirror. "If you had any sense at all," she muttered, "you'd go home! This is a man who keeps extra toothbrushes, for God's sake!"

Having said all this, Shay went back to the bedroom and crawled into bed. The sheets were as smooth as satin and the lulling motion of the water-filled mattress, coupled with the song of the tide coming in through the terrace doors, reduced her to a sleepy, languid state.

She felt the bed sway as Mitch got into it, heard the click of the lamp switch, stirred under the sweet weight of the darkness. "Are you going to make love to me?" she asked.

He chuckled and drew her close, holding her. "No," he said.

Shay yawned. "Don't let go, okay?"

"Okay," came the hoarse reply.

They both slept soundly, huddled close in that gigantic bed, neither asking anything of the other except their nearness.

Mitch awakened to an exquisite caress and opened his eyes to see a tumble-haired vamp kneeling on the bed beside him, her whole face lit by a wicked grin. "Ummm," he said, stretching, luxuriating in the pleasure she was creating. "The truce is over, I take it?"

"Every man for himself," she agreed.

"In that case . . ." He stretched again, with deceptive leisure, and then flipped over suddenly, carrying Shay with him, imprisoning her soft body beneath his own.

Her eyes widened in mock surprise and he laughed, using his nose to spar with hers.

She caught her hands together at the back of his neck and drew him into her kiss; it was a soft, nurturing thing, and yet it sent aching waves of desperate need crashing through him. He sensed that she was exerting some tender vengeance for the way he'd pleasured her in the RV the day before and he was all for it.

When the opportunity afforded itself some moments later, Mitch pulled back far enough to rid Shay of the pajama top and then fell to her again, settling against her but reluctant to take her.

Suddenly she parted her legs and the warmth of her was too compelling to be resisted. He entered her almost involuntarily, thrust into the agonizing comfort she offered by the strength of her hands and the upward thrust of her hips.

She guided him, she taunted him, she rendered him mindless with need. For all Shay's beautiful treachery, however, her moment came first and Mitch marveled at the splendor in her face as she cried out, tossing her head back and forth on the pillow and grasping at his shoulders with her hands.

"I love you," he said.

It was clear enough that Ivy's feelings were hurt. Entering the office, after a hasty shower and change of clothes at home, Shay remembered her promise to have lunch with her friend the day before and was chagrined, even though there had been no time to go out to eat.

"Hi," she said, standing before Ivy's desk.

Ivy kept her eyes on her computer screen. "Hi," she said remotely.

"Free for lunch?"

Ivy looked up quickly, and the clouds separated, revealing the sunlight that was integral to her nature. "We might have to stay in. I got kind of behind yesterday."

Shay was relieved that no permanent damage had been done to this most cherished friendship. Ivy might be nosy, but it was only because she cared so much. "We could always call Screaming Hernando's and have them send over a guacamole pizza."

Ivy made a face and then giggled.

The morning went smoothly, and when noon came, Ivy and Shay were able to slip away, Ivy having set the office answering machine to pick up any incoming calls. They had chicken sandwiches at the coffee shop across the street.

"I thought you were mad at me," Ivy confided between delicate bites from her sandwich. "I guess I shouldn't have called Mitch and told him you were filming another commercial."

Shay leaned forward, forgetting her sandwich. "So that was how he knew. I should have guessed. Ivy Prescott, what possessed you?"

"Actually," Ivy replied, "it wasn't anything quite as dramatic as possession. It was plain old bribery. Mitch promised to try to get along with my mother if I would call him whenever you were doing a spot."

"Traitor!"

"What can I tell you? I love my mother and I love Mitch and I want to see them bury the hatchet, especially with the wedding coming up."

Shay remembered what Mitch had told her the night before, when they were talking about hang-ups. "Is it working?"

"They've been civil to each other," Ivy said, shrugging. "I guess that's a start. So, are you and Mitch an item, or what?"

"An 'item'? Have you been reading old movie magazines or something?"

Ivy executed a mock glare. "Stop hedging, Shay. You don't need to tell me, you know. You can just sit by and see me consumed by my own curiosity."

Shay sighed. "If you're talking about the love-and-marriage kind of item, we're not."

Ivy's eyes were wide with delight. "That's what they all say," she replied. "So the gossip is true! You and Mitch are doing more than working together!"

"Now that is definitely none of your business, Ivy Prescott," Shay said firmly. "And exactly what gossip is this?"

"Well, you two were inside the RV together for quite a while yesterday...."

Shay willed herself not to blush at the memory and failed. She hoped Ivy would ascribe the high color in her face to righteous indignation. "What were you doing, standing out there with a stopwatch?"

"Of course not!" Ivy's feathers were ruffled. She squirmed in her chair and looked incensed and then said defensively, "I don't even own a stopwatch!"

Chapter Seven

This is some pile of bricks,'' Ivan announced, gazing appreciatively up at the walls of the house while Mitch was still recovering from the surprise of finding his agent standing on his doorstep. "Pretty big for one person, isn't it?"

Mitch stepped back to admit the small, well-dressed man with the balding pate. Ignoring Ivan's question, he offered one of his own. "What's so important that it couldn't have been handled by telephone, Ivan?"

Ivan patted his breast pocket and grinned. "An advance check of this size warrants personal delivery," he answered.

Mitch turned and walked back toward the library where he'd been working over his notes for the Rosamond Dallas book, leaving Ivan to follow. Mrs. Carraway, who had been upstairs cleaning most of the morning, magically appeared with coffee and warm croissants.

Once the pleasant-faced woman had gone, Ivan helped himself to a cup of coffee and a croissant. "Nice to see you living the good life at last, Prescott. I was beginning to think you were going to spend the rest of your days crawling through jungles on your belly and hobnobbing with the Klan."

Despite his sometimes abrasive manner, Mitch liked and respected Ivan Wright. The man was always direct, and he played hardball in all his dealings. "I guess I'm ready to settle down," he said, and his mind immediately touched on Shay.

"That could be good, and it could be bad," Ivan replied. "What are your plans for after?"

"After what?"

"After you finish the Rosamond Dallas book." Ivan added jam and cream to his croissant.

"I haven't made any plans for another project, if that's what you're getting at. I may retire. After all, I'm a rich man."

"You're also a young man," Ivan pointed out. "What are you, thirty-seven, thirty-eight?" Without waiting for an answer, the agent went on. "Your publishers want another book, Mitch, and they're willing to pay top dollar to get your name on the dotted line."

The thought made Mitch feel weary. He was having a hard enough time working up enough enthusiasm to write about Rosamond, but he supposed that was because of Shay. No matter how delicately the project was handled, she would, to some degree, be hurt by it. "We're talking about a specific subject here, I assume."

Ivan nodded, licking a dab of cream from one pudgy finger. "You've heard of Alan Roget, haven't you? That serial murderer the FBI picked up in Oklahoma a few months back?"

Mitch remembered. The man had been arraigned on some thirty-two counts of homicide. "Sweet guy," he reflected.

"Roget may be a pyscho, but he's a fan of yours. If anybody writes his story, he wants it to be you."

"They don't need his permission to do a book," Mitch pointed out, and he remembered saying a similar thing to Shay.

"No," Ivan agreed readily, calmly. "The difference is that he's willing to talk to you, tell you the whole disgusting saga from his point of view. Another writer could do the job, of course, but they'd be operating on guesswork."

"What about my anonymity? How could we trust this maniac to respect that?"

"He wouldn't have to know your real name. That can be handled, Mitch, in the same way we've handled it in the past. What do you say?" A master of timing, Ivan waited a moment and then laid the sizable check Mitch and Shay would share on the coffee table between them.

"I need time to think, Ivan. For one thing, I'm not sure I even want to hear all the rot this space-case probably plans to spill."

"Going soft, Prescott?"

"Maybe."

Ivan gave a delicate sigh and stood up. "Well, I've got a cab waiting. Got to get back to the airport, you know."

Mitch only shook his head. He was half Ivan's age, but even in his jungle-crawling, Klan-breaking days, he hadn't lived at the pace that Ivan did.

"You'll call?" Ivan asked, tugging at the jacket of his Brooks Brothers' suit to straighten it.

"I'll call." Mitch sighed the words.

Shay raised one eyebrow when Ivy informed her that the bank was calling. She couldn't be overdrawn, could she? She'd just deposited the bonus check Marvin had signed before he left, making payment for the four commercials.

"Ms. Kendall?"

Shay drew a deep breath and set aside the stack of paperwork, also left behind by Marvin, that she'd been wading through. "Yes?"

"My name is Robert Parker and I'm calling in reference to your account."

Shay tensed and then willed herself to relax. She had balanced her checkbook only a few days before, and her figures had tallied with the bank's. "Yes?"

"It seems that a sizable amount of money has been deposited and, well, we were just wondering if a mistake had been made. This sum is well beyond what the Federal Reserve will insure in any single account, you know."

"I don't understand," Shay said, resting her forehead in the palm of one hand. "Surely a four thousand dollar bonus check—"

"Four thousand dollars?" The bank officer laughed nervously. "My, my, this deposit is many times that amount. I was certain that there had to be some error."

Shay was a little stung that the banker could be so incredulous, even though she was incredulous herself.

Maybe she'd never had more than eight hundred dollars in her account at any one time, but she wasn't a deadbeat and if she'd been overdrawn a time or two, why, that had been accidental. "Wait just a moment, Mr. Parker, wasn't it? Where did this deposit come from?"

"The check itself was drawn on the account of a Mr. Mitch Prescott."

It was a moment before Shay remembered the book she and Mitch were supposed to be writing together; her mind hadn't exactly been on the professional aspects of their relationship. "Then the money is mine," she said, as much to herself as to Mr. Parker. "Would you mind telling me the exact amount?"

The sum Mr. Parker replied with made the pit of Shay's stomach leap and sent her head into a dizzying spin. Mitch had told her that her share would be a "lot" of money, but never in Shay's wildest dreams had she expected so much.

"We'll have to verify this, of course," Parker said stiffly, seeming to find Shay's good fortune suspect in some way.

"Of course," Shay answered. And then she hung up the receiver, folded her arms on the desktop and lowered her head to them.

She was rich.

The more Mitch thought about the Alan Roget project, the more it appealed to him. It would be a study in human ugliness, that book, but for once in his life he had something to counterbalance that. He had Shay.

Eager now to get the Rosamond Dallas book behind him, he unpacked his computer equipment and the attending paraphernalia and brought the machine on-line.

Working from his notes and the tapes containing Shay's observations about her mother, he began composing a comprehensive outline of the material he had on hand.

He was interrupted, at intervals, by the telephone. Mrs. Carraway tried to field his calls, but there were several that could not be avoided, one from a pedantic bank clerk questioning the deposit he'd made to Shay's account after Ivan had left, one from his daughter, Kelly, who wanted to tell him that she could visit over Christmas vacation, and one from Lucetta White. Lucetta had heard, through the grapevine, that he'd landed a "plum" of an assignment and asked for details. Mitch had talked for fifteen minutes and told Ms. White exactly nothing.

He was sitting back in his desk chair, his hands cupped behind his head, when the telephone rang again. To spare Mrs. Carraway the problem, he answered it himself with a crisp "Hello?"

"Hello," Shay replied, and the single word resounded with bewilderment. "About that money..."

Mitch waited for her to go on, but she didn't, so he replied, "Your share, as agreed. Is anything wrong?"

"Wrong? Well, no, of course not. A-are we working tonight?"

"I'm working. From now on, your part will be an occasional consultation. Of course, I'll need you to read over the material, too, as I write it."

"Oh," she said, and she sounded disappointed. Perhaps even a little hurt.

"Shay, what's the matter?"

She sighed. "I feel a little—a little superfluous, I guess. And overpaid for it in the bargain."

Mitch laughed. "You could never be superfluous, my love. Listen, if you want a more active part in writing the book, you can have it."

He could almost see her shaking her beautiful, leonine head. "No, no. I have things of my own to do, now that I'm a woman of means."

Mitch arched an eyebrow, not sure he liked the sound of that. "Like what?"

"Oh, getting solid financial advice, talking to the tax people, starting my catering service. Things of that nature."

Mitch hadn't known that Shay had aspirations to go into business for herself and he was a little peeved that she'd failed to confide something so important. He scowled down at his watch and saw that it was nearly five o'clock. "I won't keep you, then," he said stiffly, and even as he spoke the words he wondered what it was that made him want to put space between himself and this woman when he needed her so much.

There was a brief silence, and then Shay answered, "No. Well, thank you." She hung up and Mitch sat glaring at the receiver in his hand.

No. Well, thank you, he mimicked in his mind. She had what she wanted now, the money; apparently their lovemaking and the special rapport they'd formed weren't important anymore. Mitch hung up with a bang that was no less satisfying for Shay's not hearing it.

As Shay wandered up and down the aisles of the public library that evening, choosing books on the operation of small businesses, she was awash in a numbing sort of despair. All of her dreams were suddenly coming true, or, at least, most of them, and she should have been happy. She hugged the stack of self-help books close to her chest. Why wasn't she happy?

She knew the answer, of course and was only torturing herself with the question. She had thought she meant something to Mitch Prescott and found out differently. She had provided the research material he needed for his book and he'd paid her and, as far as he was concerned, the transaction was complete. There would be a few "consultations," and he wanted her input as the book progressed, but he'd made it clear enough that she wasn't to expect anything more.

Shay drove home slowly, heated a can of soup for her supper and immersed herself in the books she had checked out at the library, making notes in a spiral notebook as she read. It wasn't as though she needed Mitch Prescott to be happy, she told herself during frequent breaks in her concentration. She had Hank, she had her job, and she had the money and the determination to make her life what she'd always dreamed it could be.

Well, almost what she'd dreamed it could be.

For the rest of that week, Shay concentrated on her job at Reese Motors, grateful that she would have a little time before she had to do another commercial. She talked to Hank frequently by telephone and visited Rosamond every afternoon. From the convalescent home she invariably went to the public library, exchanging the books she'd scanned the night before for new ones. She told herself that she was preparing for her own entry into the world of private enterprise and she was learning a great deal, but the main reason for her marathon study fests was Mitch Prescott. Being absorbed in business theories kept her from thinking about him.

By Saturday morning, she was haggard. Ivy, showing up on her doorstep bright and early, was quick to point that out.

Shay yawned, feeling rumpled and dissolute in her old chenille bathrobe. "How do you expect me to look at nine o'clock on a Saturday morning? Don't you ever sleep in?"

The weather was nice and Ivy looked disgustingly vibrant in her old blue jeans and summery cotton blouse. "Sleep in?" she chimed. "And let the world pass me by?"

"The world wouldn't dare pass you by," Shay responded dryly, staggering toward the kitchen, homing in on the coffeepot which, blessedly, operated on a small timer set the night before. "Where's Todd?"

Ivy settled herself in a chair at Shay's table, shoving aside the current stack of business books with a slight frown. "He's working. Ambition is his curse, you know." She stopped for a breath. "I'm going to this great auction today. Want to come along?"

Shay poured coffee for herself and Ivy and stumbled over to the table to collapse into a chair. "Why would I want to go to an auction?"

"To buy something, silly. This is an estate sale, and they're holding it in a barn."

"I'm not in the market for harnesses and milk stools," Shay muttered, beginning to come alive as caffeine surged through her veins.

"The newspaper ad says they have a lot of great stuff, Shay. Antiques."

"Milk stools."

"You're impossible. I bought my brass bed at a sale like this, and for a song, too."

"They probably just wanted you to stop singing."

"Very funny. Come on, Shay, come with me. For the drive. For the fresh air. Good Lord, you look terrible."

Shay knew she couldn't face another day of studying. Maybe it would be fun to poke through a lot of junk in some old barn and then treat Ivy to lunch. "You haven't asked me why I look terrible, Ivy. For you, that's a drastic oversight."

Ivy sat up very straight and smiled. "I haven't asked because I already know. You and Mitch are on the outs."

"You're pleased about that?"

"I know it's temporary. Now, are you going to the sale with me or not?"

"I'm going. Just let me finish my coffee."

"No." Ivy shook her head. "They sell coffee at the sale. They sell it in little stands along the road. They sell it everywhere. Take your shower and let's go!"

Muttering, Shay abandoned her coffee and made her way to the bathroom.

The carousel horse stood, its once-bright paint chipped and faded, in the middle of the barn where the auction would be held, as though waiting for Shay.

She drew in her breath and moved toward it, her eyes wide. It couldn't be Clydesdale!

Shay crouched to look at the horse's right rear hoof. Sure enough, splotches of Rosamond's favorite fire-engine red fingernail polish still clung to the wood. The marks had been made one glum and rainy afternoon in the long-ago, by Shay herself.

Another woman came to look at the horse. "Wouldn't that make a marvelous planter, Harold?"

she was saying. "We could strip off the paint and then varnish it...."

Shay put down an urge to slap the woman away and glanced back over one shoulder at Ivy, who was inspecting a sterling-silver butter dish, one of hundreds of items set out on portable display tables.

The carousel horse, like the playhouse, had been a gift from Riley, before his divorce from Rosamond, and Shay had cherished it. The piece was valuable, and, after shipping Shay off to a summer camp, Rosamond had sold it on a whim.

The anger came back to Shay—or maybe it had never left. In any case, it was all she could do not to fling one arm over the neck of that battered, beloved old horse and cling to it, fending off all prospective buyers with her purse.

"That's nice," Ivy said suddenly from beside Shay, her eyes moving over the hand-carved and painted relic. "Are you going to bid on it?"

The woman and Harold were still standing nearby, pondering their plans to make a planter of Shay's horse. "I might," she said through tight lips, shrugging to give her words an air of indifference and nonchalance.

By the time the bidding finally began, Shay was in a state of anxiety, though she managed to appear calm. When Clydesdale—Garrett and Shay had considered a multitude of names for the horse before coming up with that one—came on the docket, she waited until the auctioneer had gotten a number of bids before entering one of her own.

Harold and the missus drove the price well beyond what Riley had paid for the piece originally, and it had been expensive then, but Shay didn't care. When the competition fell away and hers was the highest bid, she had to choke back a shout of triumph.

"What are you going to do with that, Shay?" Ivy whispered, sounding honestly puzzled.

It was a reasonable question. While Hank would consider the horse an interesting addition to their hodge-podge decorating scheme, he would not see it as a spinner of magic. "I'll explain later," Shay whispered back.

Ivy shrugged and jumped into the bidding for the silver butter dish. Later, after Shay had written a check and arranged for the horse to be delivered, she posed her original question.

Settled into the passenger seat of Ivy's car, Shay shrugged self-consciously. "He was mine, once. One of my mother's husbands gave him to me when I was a little girl. I'd just had my tonsils out, and Riley wanted to spoil me."

"Oh," said Ivy, in a fondly sentimental tone. "That's sweet."

They stopped for a late lunch and Shay was ravenous, but she was also anxious to get home. The horse would be delivered around six o'clock that evening, and she wanted to have sandpaper and fresh paints ready.

In fact, she did. She had newspapers spread out on her living room floor, too, and the deliverymen made jokes about that as they set the beloved old toy on the paper and unwrapped the blankets that had protected it.

Shay smiled wanly at their attempt at humor and had to restrain herself from shooing them out so that she could begin the restoration project. Once they'd been given their tip, they left.

Gently, Shay applied a special paint-stripping compound to the horse, removing as much of the scratched and faded finish as she could. Then she sanded. And sanded. And sanded.

It was therapy, she said to herself. She would restore Clydesdale to his former glory and when she opened her catering service, he would stand in the office, where customers could admire him. Maybe he would even become her personal insignia, his image emblazoned on her letterhead....

Letterhead. Shay smiled and shook her head. Before there could be letterhead, there had to be a business, didn't there?

As she knelt beside the carousel horse, sanding away what remained of the silver paint on one hoof, Shay felt real trepidation. It wouldn't be easy to hand in her resignation; while she could go no further in her job at Reese Motors, it was a secure position and it paid decently. The work might be trying sometimes, but it was never dull, and Marvin and Jeannie had been so kind to her.

On the other hand, Shay had money now, and a chance to follow her dreams. How many people got an opportunity like this? she asked herself. How many?

Shay sanded more vigorously, so intent on her task and her quandary that, when the doorbell rang, she was startled. Rubbing her hands down the front of an old cotton work shirt that Eliott had left behind, she got to her feet and hurried to answer the persistent ringing.

Mitch Prescott was standing on the worn doormat, looking both exasperated and contrite. He was wearing a white T-shirt and jeans, his hands wedged into his hip pockets.

Shay's heart slid over one beat and then steadied. She was painfully conscious of her rumpled hair and solvent-scented clothes. "Yes?" she said with remarkable calm.

"Dammit, Shay," he grumbled. "Let me in."

Shay stepped back and Mitch opened the screen door and came inside the now-cluttered living room. His dark eyes touched on the carousel horse, now stripped nearly to bare wood, but he made no comment.

Remembering his coolness on the telephone, Shay was determined to keep a hold on her composure, such as it was. She wasn't about to let Mitch know how his disinterest had hurt her. "May I help you?" she asked stiffly.

He looked patently annoyed. "I came here to apologize," he snapped. "Though I'm not exactly sure what it was that I did wrong."

Coolness be damned. Shay simmered, and her voice came out in a furious hiss. "You made love to me, Mitch Prescott. You laughed with me and you held me and you listened to my deepest secrets! Then, when you'd found out all you wanted to know about my mother, when you'd paid me for my trouble—"

Mitch's strong, beard-stubbled jawline tensed, and his coffee-colored eyes snapped. "That's not fair, Shay," he broke in. "The deal we made has nothing to do with what's going on between us."

"Doesn't it? Strange, but I noticed a definite decrease in your interest level once I'd told you about my mother and shared your bed a couple of times!"

"You think that's why I slept with you? To get the inside skinny on your mother?" He paused, made an angry sound low in his throat, and then ran one hand through his hair in frustration. "Good God, Shay, don't you see how neurotic that is?"

"Neurotic? You're calling me *neurotic?*"

His expression, in fact his whole demeanor, softened. "No. No, sweetheart. I'm not. You're probably the sanest person I know. But when it comes to intimate relationships, you've got some problems." Mitch sighed and spread his hands. "Little wonder, considering your mother's exploits and that bastard you married."

Shay wavered, not sure whether to be angry or comforted. There was something inside her that needed to believe Mitch, no matter what he said, and down that path lay risks that she couldn't take. She'd believed Eliott, after all, and she'd believed Rosamond's promises that each marriage would be the one that would last. "Don't you dare slander my mother," she whispered.

"Rosamond hurt you, Shay. You're angry. Why can't you admit that?"

"She's a poor, sick woman!" Shay cried. "How could I be angry at her? How?"

"You couldn't—not at the Rosamond of today, anyway. But that other Rosamond, the young, vital one who didn't have time for her own daughter—"

Shay whirled away, furious and afraid. "Why are you doing this to me? Why are you pushing me, pestering me? Why?"

He caught her upper arms in his hands and gently turned her to face him. "Shay, get mad. Admit that the woman hurt you, disappointed you. You're not going to be able to let go of that part of your life unless you face what you really feel."

Shay's chin quivered, but her eyes flashed as she looked up into Mitch's face. "How do you know what I feel?" she choked out. "How could anybody know what it's like to mean less than the latest tennis pro in your mother's life? Less than a racehorse, for God's sake?"

"Tell me what it's like, Shay. I'll listen."

Shay trembled. "Making mental notes for your book all the while, I'm sure! Get out of here, Mitch, leave me alone. I've told you all I can."

He gave her a slight shake. "Will you forget that damned book? I'm not talking about Rosamond, I'm talking about you, about us!"

"What about us, Mitch?" The question was a challenge, a mockery, an attempt to drive this man away before he could become important enough to Shay to hurt her. He already had become just that, of course, but there was such a thing as cutting one's losses and making a run for it. God knew, she thought frantically, Rosamond had taught her that if nothing else.

Mitch's hands fell slowly from Shay's shoulders and, once again, he looked toward the carousel horse. She sensed that he knew all about Clydesdale.

After a long time, Mitch sighed and started toward the door. In the opening, he paused, his eyes searching Shay's face for a moment and then shifting away. "You know, I really thought we'd be able to communicate, you and I. I really thought we had a chance."

Shay's throat tightened and tears burned in her eyes. She turned away from Mitch and took up her sandpaper.

"You can't bring back your childhood, Shay," he said, and then the door closed quietly behind him.

Shay wiped her eyes on the sleeve of her work shirt and sanded harder.

Chapter Eight

Shay stood back from the carousel horse, her hands on her hips, her head tilted to one side. She had been working on the project every night for a week and now it was done: Clydesdale was restored to his former pink, silver and pale blue glory. He looked fabulous.

She sighed, wiping her hands on her shirt. Now what was she going to do to keep herself from going mad? Hank wouldn't be home for another ten days and Shay couldn't stand the thought of reading another book on the management of a small business. She'd reached her saturation point when it came to studying. Besides, she had learned the rudiments of free enterprise by working for Marvin Reese; it was time to take real action.

Shay glanced at the clock on the wall above the TV and grimaced. It was nearly two in the morning, and the third commercial was scheduled for nine-fifteen. If she didn't get some sleep, she would never get through it.

Though Shay kept herself as busy as she possibly could, teetering always on the brink of utter exhaustion, she dreaded lying down in bed and closing her eyes. When she did, she always saw Mitch on the inner screen of her mind, heard him saying that she couldn't bring back her childhood.

She turned her gaze to the beautiful wooden horse and wondered why anyone would want to bring back a childhood like hers. There had been so many disappointments, so many tears; she'd lived in luxurious neglect, having about as much access to Rosamond as any other adoring fan.

Shay bit her lower lip and shook her head in an effort to curtail that train of thought. No, Mitch Prescott had been wrong: she had no desire to relive those little-girl days. Clydesdale was merely a pleasant reminder that there had been happy, whimsical times, as well as painful ones.

With one hand, Shay tried to rub away the crick in her neck and started off toward the bathroom, looking forward to a hot, soothing shower. But she paused and looked back and it occurred to her that Clydesdale might not be just a memento—he might be a sort of emotional Trojan horse.

"May I say that you look absolutely dreadful?" Richard Barrett asked as Shay riffled through the mail on her office desk and picked out a postcard from Jeannie and Marvin. There was a picture of the Eiffel Tower on the front of the card, and Shay felt a pang at the thought of telling the Reeses about her decision to resign and start her own business.

"You have bags under your eyes, for God's sake!" Richard persisted.

Shay smiled ruefully and reread the almost illegible script on the back of the postcard. The Reeses would be home in another week and a half; she would break the news to them once they'd had time to get over their jet lag and settle in. "That gives me an idea," she teased, enjoying Richard's annoyance over the smudges that betrayed her lack of sleep. "For a commercial, I mean. You could show me, close up, and I could say, 'Come down to Reese Motors and bag yourself a good deal!' Get it, Richard? *Bag* yourself a good deal?"

"You're not only exhausted, you're insane. Shay, what's the matter with you?"

"Nothing a half ton of sugar wouldn't cure. This is Sugar Day, isn't it, Richard?"

Richard had the good grace to look just a little shamefaced. "Yes. Shay, it's safe, really. I wouldn't ask you to do anything dangerous."

"By all means, let's confine ourselves to the merely ridiculous."

Mr. Barrett sighed dramatically and flung up his hands. "You knew what doing these commercials entailed, Shay, and you agreed to it all!"

"At the time, I needed the money."

"Are you trying to back out of the deal?" Richard's voice was a growl.

Shay shook her head. "No. When I make a promise, I keep it. Even when it means making a fool of myself." Her association with Mitch Prescott and his stupid book, she added, to herself, was a case in point.

"Well, let's get this over with before it rains or something. I've got a dump-truck load of sugar down there waiting." Richard looked truly beleaguered. "I'll be just as glad when that last commercial is in the can as you will, you know!" he barked.

"Nobody could possibly be that glad, Richard," Shay replied tartly. "Now get out of my office, will you please? I need some time to prepare for my big scene."

Richard muttered a single word as he left. It might have been "witch," but Shay wasn't betting on it.

The moment she was alone, she punched the button on her intercom. "Ivy? Would you get Todd on the phone, please?"

Instead of giving her answer over the wire, Ivy dashed into the office to demand in person, "Why? Shay, what are you planning to do?"

Shay sank into her desk chair with a sigh. Because she didn't have the strength to spar with Ivy, she answered readily. "I've decided that it's time to step out on my own, Ivy. I'm going to open my catering business and I'll need a place to work from."

Ivy's expression revealed two distinct and very different emotions: admiration and disappointment. "Wow," she said.

"Make the call, Ivy," Shay replied briskly, shuffling papers around on her desk in a pretense of being too busy to talk.

Five minutes later Todd was on the line. He listened to Shay's comments on the sort of building she needed and, bless him, asked no personal questions whatsoever. He had two good prospects, in fact: a Victorian house on Hill Street and a small restaurant overlooking the ocean. Both were available for lease with options to buy, and both had been abandoned for a considerable length of time.

Shay smiled into the telephone receiver. "You're telling me that they're fixer-uppers, aren't you, Todd?"

Todd laughed. "Yes, but the prices are right. Do you want to look at them?"

"Oh, yes, and as soon as possible."

"How about tonight, after you get off work?"

Despite her weariness, Shay felt a thrill of excitement. After all, she was doing something she had only dreamed about before: she was starting her own business. "That will be great. Why don't we make an evening of it? I'll order a pizza and throw together a salad and you and Ivy can have dinner with me."

"Sounds terrific," Todd agreed warmly. "See you at five."

"Five-thirty would be better. I've got a commercial to do this morning, and that always makes me fall behind on everything else."

"Five-thirty, then," Todd confirmed.

To save Ivy the trouble of an inquisition, Shay went out to her desk and relayed the plan. Ivy, who loved any sort of get-together no matter how casual or how highbrow, was delighted.

Chuckling, Shay started toward the stairs, ready for the third commercial. On the top step, she paused and turned to look back at her friend. "Don't you dare call your brother, either!"

Ivy beamed, sitting up very straight behind her computer terminal. "Too late!" she sang back.

Shay's hopeful mood faded instantly. She glared at her friend and stomped down the metal stairs to meet her singular and ignoble fate.

The dump truck was parked in the rear lot, as Richard had said, and the camera people were checking angles. Surreptitiously, Shay looked around as she walked toward the RV allotted for her use. If Mitch was there, she didn't see him.

This time her makeup was simple; merely a heavier version of what she normally wore. She shooed Richard's chattering assistant out of the RV and got ready, leaving the coveralls she would wear for last.

Outside—thank heaven, there was still no sign of Mitch—she read off the list of special car deals Marvin had authorized before his departure for Europe and then braced herself as the clapboard snapped and the cameras focused on her and on the dump truck parked nearby.

Smiling brightly, she announced, "Come on down to Reese Motors, folks! We guarantee you a sweet deal!"

On cue, the back of the dump truck ground upward and an avalanche of white sugar cascaded down onto Shay, burying her completely. She fought her way to the surface, sputtering and coughing, silently vowing that she would kill Richard Barrett if he wasn't satisfied with the first take.

"It's a wrap!" Richard shouted joyously and a laughing cheer went up from the salesmen, who had, as usual, gathered to watch.

Shay's hair and eyelashes were full of sugar. It filled her shoes, like sand, and even made its way under her clothes to chafe against her skin. She vowed she'd never put the stuff in her coffee again as she hurried back toward the RV, desperate to shower and change her clothes.

She began ripping them off the moment she'd closed the door behind her, flinging them in every direction. When the RV's engine suddenly whirred to life and the vehicle lurched into motion, she was stark naked.

Her first thought was that the salesmen were playing some kind of prank. Half amused and half furious, she wrenched a blanket from the bed above the RV's cab and wrapped it around herself.

"Stop!" she yelled.

The RV stopped, but only for a second. It was soon swinging into mid-morning traffic. Just when Shay would have screamed, a familiar masculine voice called from the front, "Don't worry, it's all arranged! You have the day off!"

Too furious to think about the fact that she was crusted with white sugar and wrapped in a blanket, Shay flung aside the little curtain that separated the cab of the RV from the living quarters and raged, "Mitch Prescott, you stop this thing right now! I'm getting out!"

He looked back at her, his mouth serious, his eyes laughing. "In this traffic? Woman, are you mad? You'd make the six o'clock news, and if you think the commercials were embarrassing..."

"You'll be the one who makes the news, bucko!" Shay screamed, outraged. "This is not only kidnapping, it's grand theft auto!"

"I'll have you know that I rented this rig," he answered calmly.

"Well, you didn't rent me! Turn this thing around, now!"

"I'd need a football field to do that, sweets," came the happily resigned reply. "We're in this for twenty-four hours, plus mileage, I'm afraid."

"You idiot! You—you *caveman*—" Shay paused, breathless, and looked around for something to throw.

"I like the idea of dragging you off to a cave, I must admit," Mitch reflected good-naturedly. "It's the whacking you over the head with a club and hauling you off by the hair that I can't quite deal with."

"You'd never prove that by me!"

Mitch laughed and someone honked as he switched lanes to fly up a freeway ramp. Shay gave a choked little cry and slumped down on the floor in a bundle of sugared synthetic wool. There, she considered her options.

Jumping out of a vehicle traveling at fifty-five miles per hour was definitely out. So was putting her clothes back on without showering first, and she couldn't face the thought of taking a shower with this maniac at the wheel.

A sweet, throbbing warmth moved beneath Shay's skin as she reviewed her situation. There were worse things than being alone with Mitch Prescott, whatever their differences. "Was Ivy in on this?"

"I'm pleading the fifth on that one, sugar plum."

Just the mention of sugar made Shay itch all over. She squirmed in her blanket and wailed, "When I get my hands on her—"

There was, for the first time since that crazy ride had begun, a serious note in Mitch's voice. "We have to talk, Shay."

"You didn't have to kidnap me for that!"

"Didn't I? The last time I tried, you were something less than receptive."

Shay yawned. It was crazy, but all her sleepless nights seemed to be catching up to her, demanding their due. Now, of all times! She curled up in her blanket and closed her eyes. The swaying, jostling motion of the RV lulled her into a languorous state of half slumber. "Why... are you... doing this?" she asked again.

She could have sworn he said it was because he loved her....

Nah. She'd only dreamed that.

Mitch paced the length of the secluded beach, his hands pushed into the hip pockets of his jeans. What had he done? Was he losing his reason? For all his exploits, he'd never stooped to anything like this. Never.

He looked back at the RV he'd taken such pains to rent and sighed a raspy sigh that grated in his throat. Shay was still asleep, he supposed. When she woke up, she was going to fly into his face like a mother eagle defending her nest. He bent and grasped a piece of driftwood in one hand, and flung it into the surf.

Maybe it was that week of twenty-hour workdays. Maybe that had shorted out his brain or something.

The door of the RV creaked open and Mitch braced himself. Shay was going to give him hell, and the knowledge that he deserved whatever she might say didn't make the scenario any easier to prepare for.

She was still wearing the blanket, and little grains of sugar glimmered like bits of crystal in her hair, in her eyebrows, on her skin. Barefoot, she made her way toward him through the clean brown sand.

"I'm sorry, Shay," he said gruffly when she finally stood facing him, her wide hazel eyes unreadable. "I don't believe I did this—"

She raised the fingers of one hand to his lips, silencing him. Hidden birds chirped in the towering pine trees that edged the beach; gulls squawked in the distance; the tide made whispery music against the shore. It was a poetic interlude where only the earth and the waters spoke.

A primitive, grinding need possessed Mitch; he wanted Shay, craved her. But he didn't dare touch her, or even speak. How was he going to explain this?

Her fingers moved from his lips to caress his jawline and then trace the length of his neck. He shuddered with the aching need of her.

You know the thrill
of escaping to a world where

Love, Romance, and Happiness reach out to one and all...

TAKE FOUR

SILHOUETTE SPECIAL EDITION® NOVELS

FREE...

Escape again ... with 4 FREE novels

Τhat's right. We'll send you all 4 Silhouette Special Edition novels (a $10.00 value), plus a *Folding Umbrella and Mystery Gift FREE*. Take:

Lisa Jackson's DEVIL'S GAMBIT. Tiffany had problems with her breeding farm long before handsome Zane Sheridan offered to buy her out. What was it in his cold grey eyes that made Tiffany so uncertain? And so convinced?

Natalie Bishop's STRING OF PEARLS. Brittany and Devon were once devoted to one another. Now, circumstances have brought them together again, perhaps on opposite sides of the law.

Patti Beckman's DATELINE: WASHINGTON. Newspaper reporter Janelle Evans saw Bart Tagert only as a rival, until a Washington scandal brought them together—and into each other's arms.

Linda Lael Miller's STATE SECRETS. Holly Llewellyn's cousin was about to become President of the United States. Secret Service agent David Goddard's interest in her was strictly professional...or was it?

After you receive your FREE books, we'll send you 6 new books to preview every month for 15 days. If you decide to keep them, pay just $11.70 (a $15.00 value) with no extra charge for home delivery. You'll also receive the Silhouette Books Newsletter FREE with every book shipment. Cancel at any time, just by dropping us a note. The first 4 books, Folding Umbrella and Mystery Gift are yours to keep in any case.

Get a FREE
Folding Umbrella
& Mystery Gift too!

Escape with 4 FREE

Silhouette Special Edition novels (a $10.00 Value) and get a Folding Umbrella & Mystery Gift, too!

"They forgot to fill the water tank," she announced.

Mitch had been expecting a glorious, violent rage, expecting anything but this inane remark. He gaped at her, and his breath sawed at his lungs as it moved in and out. "What?"

"There isn't any water for the shower," Shay answered, holding the blanket in place with one hand and stroking Mitch's neck with the other. "In the RV, I mean."

She was a constant surprise to Mitch; just when he expected her to be furious, she was quiet. Or was this just the calm before the storm? "A shower?" he echoed stupidly.

Shay's lush lips curved into a smile. "If you'd just had a half ton of sugar dumped on you, you'd want a shower, too."

His frustration doubled and redoubled. Was she tormenting him deliberately? Was she making him want her, just so she could exact revenge by denying him when his need was greatest? "Dammit, Shay, I just shanghaied you and you're standing there talking about showers! Get back in the RV and I'll take you home."

The sweet lips made a pout. "I told you," she said. "I'm covered with sugar. I can't go home like this."

It was revenge; Mitch was sure of it. He made a growling sound in his bafflement and started to turn away. She caught his arm in her small, strong hand and urged him back around to face her.

The blanket seemed to waft to the sand in slow motion and Mitch couldn't breathe, couldn't move, couldn't think.

Shay stood on tiptoe, and when her lips touched Mitch's, he was lost. He groaned and gathered her to him with both hands, her soft flesh warm and gritty beneath his palms. He lowered her to the blanket, taking no time to smooth it, his mouth desperate for hers, his hands stroking her, shaping her for the taking. But he denied himself that possession, denied her, choosing instead to break the kiss and taste Shay's sugared breasts, her stomach, her thighs.

She writhed in pleasure, tossing her head back and forth, her fingers fierce in his hair. If she was setting him up for a last-second denial, she was doing a damned good job of it; Mitch wasn't sure he'd be able to stop if she asked that of him. He felt as though he'd stumbled into some jungle river, as though he were being flung along by currents too strong to swim against.

He didn't remember taking off his clothes, but suddenly he was naked, his flesh pressed against the strange roughness of hers. In silence she commanded his entry, in obedience and passion he complied.

They moved together in a ferocious rhythm, every straining thrust of their bodies increasing the pace until they both cried out, each consumed by the other, their flesh meeting in a final quivering arch. They fell slowly from the heights, gasping, sinking deep into the warm sand.

It took some time for Shay to coerce her lax, passion-sated muscles to lift her from that tangled blanket on the sand. When she managed to stand up, she stumbled toward the surf, into it.

The water was cold, even though it was August, and the chill of it nipped at Shay's knees and thighs and hips as she waded farther out. Mitch was beside her in a moment and she smiled to think that he might be afraid for her.

Shivering, his lips blue with cold, he caught her upper arms in his hands. "Shay."

She didn't want to hear an apology. Nothing could be allowed to spoil the sweet ferocity of the minutes just past. She cupped both hands in the sea and flung salty water into Mitch's face, laughing as he cursed, lost his balance and came up sputtering with cold and fury.

Shay held her breath and submerged herself, letting the ocean wash away the last of the sugar from her body and came up to be pulled immediately into a breathless kiss.

When that ended, Mitch lifted her into his arms, carried her back onto the shore. He lowered her to the sand, the blanket forgotten, and made slow, sweet love to her. Her cries of pleasure carried high into the blue summer sky, tangling with the coarse calls of the seabirds.

"I really have to go back," Shay said quietly. She was dressed again, the dream was over. "Todd has a couple of buildings to show me."

"Buildings?" Mitch, too, was fully dressed, and he sat across the RV's tiny table from Shay, looking strangely defeated.

"I've decided to take the plunge and start my catering business."

Mitch's jaw tightened. "Oh."

"Why does that bother you so much?" Shay asked. "Despite your caveman tactics this afternoon, you don't give the impression of being a chauvinist."

"I'm not a chauvinist, dammit!" Mitch snapped, looking for all the world like a wounded and outraged little boy. "We made love, Shay. We worked together. Maybe we haven't known each other very long, but we've shared a lot. It hurt that you didn't mention something that important.''

Shay shrugged, confused. "Until you gave me that money for helping with the book, it was just a dream, Mitch. I have a child to support and I couldn't have taken the risks. What would be the point in talking about something I didn't expect to be able to do?''

There was a short silence while Mitch absorbed the things Shay had said. "I guess I did overreact a little,'' he finally admitted. His eyes met hers. "I'm sorry about this morning, too. I had no right to do that.''

"It was pretty crazy,'' Shay agreed, but she couldn't bring herself to be angry. Instead her whole being seemed to resonate with a feeling of contentment. "What made you do it?''

Mitch's broad shoulders moved in a shrug and he rubbed his beard-stubbled chin with one hand as he thought. "It was a hell of a way to show it, but I love you, Shay.''

Shay swallowed hard. She had really heard the words; this time she wasn't dreaming or so caught up in the throes of passion that she couldn't be sure she'd understood them correctly. She tried to speak and failed.

"You don't believe me?''

Shay swallowed again. "We haven't known each other very long, Mitch. Oth-other things are so good between us that—well, we could be confusing that with love, couldn't we?''

"Marry me,'' he said.

"No,'' she replied. "I can't.''

"Why not?''

"Because.''

"Oh, that's a great answer. God, I hate it when I ask someone a simple question and they say 'because'!''

Shay couldn't resist a smile, though it was a sad one. "I guess the day is over, huh?"

Mitch was glaring at her. "I guess it is. But we aren't over. Is that clear, Shay? You and I are not over."

"For a best-selling writer, you have terrible grammar. Speaking of that, how's the book going?"

"I'm halfway through the first draft," Mitch answered in clipped and somewhat grudging tones. "Why won't you marry me, Shay? Don't you love me?"

"As crazy as it seems, I think I do love you. If I didn't, I would have been on the main highway, trying to flag down a state patrolman."

"But?"

"But I've seen my mother fail at marriage over and over. I've failed at it myself. I can't go through that again, Mitch."

"If you need to prove that you can make it on your own, well, it seems to me that you've already done that."

"Have I, Mitch? Until you came along and offered me a fat fee for my help in writing that book about my mother, I was barely making it from one payday to the next. I haven't proved anything; I've just been lucky."

Mitch shook his head. "So now it's the catering business. If you make that fly, you're a valid person. Is that it, Shay?"

"I guess it is."

"Then I feel sorry for you."

The words came as a slap in the face to Shay; she sat back on the narrow bench, her eyes wide, her breath caught in her throat. "What?"

"You're in a trap, Shay. You're an intelligent woman, so you must know that the value of a person has nothing to do with what they prove or don't prove."

Shay felt distinctly uncomfortable. Next he'd be saying that she was just using her need to succeed at something to avoid taking a chance on marriage. "I suppose if we were married, you'd want me to give up the whole idea of starting a catering service."

"On the contrary, Shay, I'd help you in any way I could." He looked grimly smug. "Wriggle your way out of that one."

Shay was stumped. "Okay, so I'm afraid. It's human to be afraid when you've been hurt."

"This conversation is getting us nowhere." Mitch stood up, took the keys to the RV from the pocket of his jeans. "Can we at least agree that we'll give this relationship or whatever the hell it is a sporting chance?"

Shay could only nod.

"That's progress, at least. Let's go."

They were both settled in the front seat and the RV was jolting up the narrow road to the highway before either of them spoke again.

"I want to read what you've written so far, Mitch. About Rosamond, I mean."

Mitch did not take his eyes from the road. "Buckle your seatbelt. You're free to read the manuscript whenever you want."

Shay snapped the belt into place and sighed. "Ivy and Todd are coming over for pizza after I look at those properties. Why don't you join us?"

"Now that was an enthusiastic invitation if I've ever heard one. Are you afraid I'd end up staying the night?"

"I *know* you would end up staying the night."

Mitch cast a sidelong look at her and shook his head. "Woman, you defy logic. Caution is your middle name, and yet you seem to enjoy walking on thin ice."

"I'm as confused as you are, if that helps," Shay admitted ruefully. "Are you coming over for pizza or not?"

"I'm coming over for one hell of a lot more than pizza, lady, and you know it. Am I still invited?"

Shay thought for a long time. "Yes," she finally answered. "The invitation stands."

Chapter Nine

If Ivy and Todd were surprised when Shay arrived at Reese Motors promptly at five-thirty, they had the good grace not to show it. Freshly showered and made up, Shay went into her office long enough to check her telephone messages and align her work for the next day.

When she came out, her friends were waiting, Ivy wide-eyed and just a bit pale, Todd blithely unaware that anything was amiss.

Shay gave Ivy a scorching look that warned of an imminent confrontation and said, "Well, let's look at those buildings. We'll pick up the pizza on the way to my place, afterward."

Ivy swallowed visibly and croaked, "Okay."

Their first stop was the large Victorian house Todd had mentioned. It had been empty for a long time, but Shay could see vast potential in it; if she renovated the place, she would have room not only for her business, but for half a dozen small shops. She wouldn't run these herself, of course, but rent them to other people.

Todd assured her that the house was basically sound, though it needed a great deal of work. The plaster in most of the rooms was either stained or falling off the walls in hunks, and the ceilings sagged.

Shay liked the house; it had personality. The kitchen, while much in need of repair, was large enough to accommodate the needs of a catering service, and the spacious dining room could be converted to a reception area of sorts. The pantry, almost as big as Shay's kitchen in her rented house, would make a suitable private office.

"I have some rough estimates on the renovation, if you'd like to see them," Todd offered.

Shay was pleased by his thoroughness. Here was a man who would go far in the business world. She reviewed the estimates submitted by various construction companies as they drove to the other potential site. The amounts of money involved were staggering.

The second site was a small restaurant overlooking the water. The ceiling had fallen down, coming to rest across a counter still equipped with a cash register. Debris of every sort was scattered on the floor, seeming to pool around the bases of the tattered stools that lined the counter. The smell of mice was potent.

"It does look out over the water," Ivy ventured. She'd been very quiet all along.

"That's about all it has going for it," Shay replied. "If I were going to open a bistro or something, I might be interested, but I don't think a view is going to be any particular plus for a catering service."

Todd nodded his agreement.

Suddenly, Shay was very tired. After all, it had been a crazy day. "I'll need some time to think this over, Todd, but I'm interested in the other place. Do you think I could get back to you in a few days?"

Again, Todd nodded. "You might want to get some other estimates. The ones I gave you were meant to give an idea of what would be required."

Shay looked down at the sheaf of papers in her hand. "Do you recommend these people, Todd?"

He held the door open and Ivy sort of skulked through, just ahead of Shay. "I've dealt with all of them at one time or another and they do fine work. But you should still get other estimates, it's always good business."

They stopped at a pizza-to-go place and, as Shay waited at the counter for her order, she happened to glance through the front window. Ivy and Todd appeared to be having some kind of serious consultation in the car. Ivy's head was bent and Shay found her irritation with her friend fading away.

Ivy was a meddler extraordinaire, but she meant well. She was happy with Todd and she wanted everyone else she knew to be happy, too. Still, Shay thought the young woman deserved the lecture she was probably getting at that moment.

The pizza was ready and Shay was distracted from the scene in the car for a few moments. When she reached it, carrying the pizza, Ivy and Todd were sitting as far from each other as they possibly could. Shay let herself into the back seat, wrestling the huge pizza box as she did so and, of course, made no comment on the chill inside the car.

At Shay's house, a very subdued Ivy took over the making of the salad. When Mitch arrived she started and looked even more guilty and disconsolate than before.

Mitch gave Shay a quick kiss on the lips and turned to his sister, who tossed him a defiant look and made a face.

Mitch laughed and then reached out to rumple Ivy's gossamer hair, but he spoke to Shay. "Ivy didn't know why I wanted to rent that RV until it was too late."

Ivy startled everyone by bursting into tears and fleeing through the back door. Todd started to follow, but Shay stopped him with a gesture of one hand and a quiet "No. I'll talk to her."

She found Ivy sitting at the picnic table, her head resting on her folded arms, her small shoulders shaking.

Shay laid a hand on her friend's quivering back and said, "Hey. It's all right, Ivy. I'm not mad at you."

"I could kill that brother of mine!" Ivy wailed, sniffling intermittently. "Oh, Shay, I never thought he'd do anything like that!"

Shay couldn't help smiling a little. "No harm was done. Let's forget it."

Ivy turned and flung herself into Shay's arms for a quick hug. After that, she recovered quickly.

During dinner, served on that same picnic table, the conversation centered mostly on the house Shay was thinking of taking for her catering business and her ideas about renting out the other rooms as small shops.

Mitch said very little, but the light in his brown eyes revealed a certain amused respect that told Shay he liked the idea. Ivy, of course, was bursting with suggestions: she knew a woman who made beautiful candles and would be overjoyed to be a part of such a project, was acquainted with another who had been wanting to import Christmas ornaments to sell to the tourists as souvenirs but had had no luck in finding a shop she could afford.

When the pizza and salad were gone and the paper plates had been thrown away, Ivy and Todd made an abrupt, if cheerful, exit.

"Was it something I said?" Shay said with a frown.

Mitch grinned. "Don't be naive," he replied.

While Mitch brewed a pot of coffee, seeming as at home in Shay's kitchen as if it had been his own, she settled onto the couch with the pages of his manuscript. She had never known a writer before, but she had expected a first draft to be a mass of scribbles and cross-outs and have scrawled notes in the margins. Mitch's pages were remarkably neat and there was something in his style that grabbed Shay's attention, made her read as someone who had never met Rosamond Dallas might.

Presently, Mitch set a steaming cup on the coffee table in front of her, but she didn't pause to reach for it. She was fascinated, seeing a side of Rosamond that she hadn't consciously noticed before.

By the time she'd raced through a hundred and fifty pages of concise, perceptive copy, her coffee was cold in the cup and her view of Rosamond—and Mitch himself—had been broadened by the length of a horizon.

"Wow," she said.

Mitch took away her coffee cup, refilled it and returned to the living room. "You approve, I take it?"

"I'm not sure if I approve or not, but I'm impressed. The writing is good, Mitch, really good. How could you have learned so much about Rosamond from a few pictures and scrapbooks and a couple of conversations with me?''

Mitch was settled into the overstuffed chair nearest the couch. "I did a lot of research, Shay. For instance, I talked to all six of her ex-husbands by phone. And your grandmother—''

"My grandmother?" Shay felt a quickening inside, one of mingled surprise and alarm. "I don't have a grandmother."

Mitch lowered his eyes to his coffee, taking a sip before he answered, "Yes, you do."

Shay set the pages of the manuscript aside, fearing that she would drop them if she didn't. "Speaking of things people don't bother to mention . . ."

Mitch set aside his cup and raised both hands in a gesture of peace. "I didn't find out about her until this afternoon, Shay, after I'd dropped you off here. One of my research people had tracked her down and they left her name and phone number on my answering machine."

Shay swallowed. "You called her?"

"Yes. Her name is Alice Bretton and she lives in Springfield, Missouri. Your father—''

"Is her son," Shay's voice was shaky.

"Was her son, I'm afraid. He was a navy pilot, Shay, and he was shot down over Hanoi in 1970." Mitch was sitting beside Shay on the couch now, holding her gently and not too tightly.

"They're sure? So many pilots were taken prisoner—''

"He's dead, Shay. He was positively identified."

An overwhelming feeling of betrayal and hurt washed over Shay. "I didn't even know him. Rosamond wouldn't tell me his name."

"His name was Robert Bretton."

"Tell me about him!"

Mitch sighed. "I don't know the whole story. He and Rosamond were 'going steady,' as they called it back then. When things went wrong, your mother bought a bus ticket to Hollywood and from what Mrs. Bretton told me, Robert finished college and then joined the navy."

Shay was dizzied by the sudden influx of information that had been denied her throughout her life, first by Rosamond's reluctance to talk, then by her illness. "There are so many things I want to know...."

"Why don't you get in touch with your grandmother tomorrow? She'll be able to tell you a lot more than I can."

"She might not want anything to do with me!"

Mitch shook his head. "She asked me a thousand questions about you, Shay." He pulled a wry face meant to lighten the mood. "Of course, I didn't tell her how you taste when you've just had a half ton of sugar dumped over your head."

Shay was making a sound, but she wasn't sure whether she was laughing or crying or both. She gave Mitch a shove and then allowed her forehead to nestle into his broad shoulder.

"Make love to me, Mitch," she said after a very long time.

"Here?" he teased in a hoarse voice, but he picked Shay up in his arms and carried her into the room she pointed out to him. The night was a long one, full of tender abandon.

The pit of Shay's stomach quivered with nervousness as she dialed the number Mitch had given her.

What, exactly, was she going to say to this grand-mother she had never known, never heard a word about?

Mitch puttered around the kitchen, getting break-fast, while the call went through.

"Mrs. Bretton?" Shay's voice shook. "My name is Shay Kendall and—"

"Shay!" The name was a soft cry of joy, full of tears and laughter. "Is it really you?"

"It's really me," Shay answered, and she made a face at Mitch as he shoved a dishtowel into her hands. Then she dried her eyes with it. "T-tell me about my father. Please."

"There is so much to tell, darling, and so much to show. Could you possibly come to Springfield for a visit?"

Shay wanted to hop on the next plane, but she had responsibilities to Marvin and Jeannie and she couldn't go away without letting Hank know. Suppose he got sick and Garrett brought him home and there was no one there to take care of him? "This is a bad time—my job—my son—"

"Then I'll come there!" Alice Bretton interrupted warmly. "Would that be all right, Shay? I could bring the photo albums and we could talk in person."

"I'd love to have you, Mrs. Bretton."

"In that case, I'll make arrangements and call you right back."

"That would be wonderful."

They said goodbye and Shay set the phone receiver back in its cradle as Mitch poured scrambled eggs into a pan of hash browns and chopped onions and bits of crisp bacon.

"I take it she's flying out for a visit?" Mitch asked moderately, looking back at Shay over one bare shoulder.

Shay nodded. "I can't make sense of what I feel, Mitch. I'm happy that I'm finally going to meet my grandmother and I'm sad because my father died and I'm furious with Rosamond! Here she is, this poor, sick, wretch of a woman, and I could cheerfully wring her neck!"

"That's normal, Shay. The important thing is that you wouldn't really do it."

"I want to thank you for this, Mitch. F-for my grandmother."

He turned from the stove, grinning, almost unbearably handsome in just his jeans. His hair was rumpled and his feet were bare and, as always, he needed to shave. "Don't be too hasty with your gratitude, kid," he warned. "For all you know, she's a bag lady with bad breath, bunions and bowling shoes."

"That was alliterative, in a tacky sort of way," Shay responded. She slid off the stool near the wall phone and put her arms around Mitch's lean waist.

He kissed the tip of her nose and gave her bottom a squeeze that brought back memories of the night before. Shay blushed to recall what a greedy wanton she'd been.

"I'm not sure whether you bring out the best in me, or the worst," she commented.

Mitch's eyebrows went into brief but rapid motion. "If that was your worst," he said in a Groucho Marx voice, "I'm all for it."

Shay tipped her head back and laughed. It was a throaty, gleeful sound, and it felt oh, so good. If she could be sure that life with Mitch Prescott would always be this way, she would have married him in a second. But in her deepest mind, marriage was linked with betrayal, with pain. She sobered, thinking of Eliott's desertion and the fickle vanity of her mother.

Mitch lifted his index fingers to the corners of Shay's mouth and stretched her lips into a semblance of a smile. "No sad faces allowed," he said.

He went to dish up the scrambled egg concoction he'd made for their breakfast, and Shay sat down in a chair at the table. It was strange, having a man not only cook for her, but serve her as well. "I could get used to this," she said as he set a steaming, fragrant plate in front of her.

"Good. We'll get married and make it a ritual. I'll fix your breakfast every morning and then take you back to bed and make wild love to you."

Shay blushed again, but some vixen hiding deep inside her made her say, "Keep making threats like that, fella, and I'll accept your proposal."

Mitch's eyes were suddenly serious. "Eat," he ordered in a gruff tone, looking away.

Before Shay could say anything at all, the telephone rang. Alice Bretton had made her flight arrangements and she would be arriving in Seattle the following afternoon at two. Shay wrote down the name of the airline and the flight number and when she turned away from the phone, Mitch was disconsolately scraping their plates.

Standing behind him, Shay wrapped her arms around his middle and rubbed his stomach with tantalizing motions of both hands. "I seem to remember something about a threat," she said softly, her lips moving against the taut flesh of his back as she spoke.

Shay was late for work that morning.

Just talking to Alan Roget over the telephone gave Mitch a creepy feeling, as though a massive spiderweb had settled over him or something. He frowned as he listened to the first accounts of the murderer's child-hood, entering notes on the screen of his computer throughout the conversation.

The night with Shay had been magical, and so had the morning. Life was so damned ironic: one minute, a man could be eating scrambled eggs or making love to a woman, the next, talking to someone who personified evil. Like most psychotics, Roget exhibited no remorse at all, from what Mitch could tell. He seemed to feel that civil and moral laws applied only to other people and not to him.

By the time Mitch hung up the telephone, he was a little sick. He immediately dialed Reba's number in California, and when she answered, he asked to talk to Kelly.

"You're in luck, big fella," Reba responded warmly. "The munchkin happens to be home from school to-day."

Mitch sat up a little straighter in his desk chair. "Is she sick?"

"Nothing serious," his ex-wife assured him promptly. "Just the sniffles. So, how have you been, Mitch?"

Mitch couldn't help smiling. Reba definitely wasn't your standard ex-wife. She was happy with her new husband and that happiness warmed her entire person-ality. "I'm in love," he confided, without really expecting to.

"Oh, Mitch, that's great!" Worry displaced a little of the buoyancy in her voice. "It *is* great, isn't it? Maybe great enough to keep you out of jungles and hotbeds of political unrest?"

"No more jungles, Reba," he said solemnly. He'd made changes in his life recently that he had refused to consider while he and Reba were married, and he wondered if she would resent that.

Not Reba. He should have known. "We'll all breathe a sigh of relief," she chimed. "On the count of three, now. One, two—"

Mitch laughed. He remembered the good times with Reba and, for a fleeting moment, mourned them.

When Kelly's piping voice came on the line, he forget about Roget and all the other ugliness in the world. But the house seemed even bigger than it was after he'd talked to his daughter, and even emptier.

He threw himself into his work, concentrating on Rosamond Dallas and what had made her tick.

The need to throttle Rosamond was gone by the time Shay visited her that afternoon; in its place was a certain sad acceptance of the fact that mothers are women, human and fallible.

She approached her mother's chair, kissed her forehead. "How can I hate you?" she whispered.

Rosamond rocked and clutched the ever-present doll. It seemed to Shay that she was retreating deeper and deeper into herself and growing smaller with every passing day.

Tired because of a most delicious lack of sleep the night before, a day of work and telephone conversations with half a dozen contractors, Shay sighed and sank into the chair facing her mother's. "I'm going to meet my grandmother tomorrow," she said, hardly able to believe such a thing could be possible and expecting no reaction at all from Rosamond.

But the woman sat stiffly in her chair, her famous eyes widening.

Shay was incredulous. "Mother?"

The fleeting moment of lucidity was over. Rosamond stared blankly again, crooning a wordless song to her doll.

Shay looked at the doll and, for the first time ever, wondered if that raggedy lump of cloth and yarn could, in Rosamond's mind, represent herself as a baby. It was a jarring thought, but oddly comforting, too. Maybe, Shay thought, she loved me as well as she was able to love anyone. Maybe she did the best she could.

On her way home from the convalescent home, Shay stopped at the Skyler Beach mall and went into a bookstore, looking for the four titles Ivy had written down for her. Mitch's work was published under the odd code name of Zebulon, with no surname of any kind given and, of course, with no photograph on the back or inside flap of the book jackets.

Shay felt a little shiver of fear as she looked at the covers and thought of all the dangerous people who must hate Mitch Prescott enough to kill him. She was trembling a little as she laid the books on the counter and paid for them.

At home, she did housework, ate a light supper and took a bath, then curled up on the couch with one of Mitch's books. The one she'd selected to read first was an account of the capture of a famous Nazi war criminal, set mostly in Brazil. It was harrowing, reading that book, and yet Shay was riveted to it, turning page after page. In the morning, she awakened to find herself still on the couch, the open book under her cheek. Groaning, she raised herself to a sitting position and ran her fingers through her hair.

This was the day that she would meet Alice Bretton, her grandmother, for the first time. She was determined to think of that and not the horrors Mitch had to have faced in order to write that book.

After showering and dressing, she wolfed down a cup of coffee and half an English muffin and drove to work to find the usual chaos awaiting her. At least Richard Barrett wasn't around, wanting to film the last commercial. That was a comfort.

Shay delved into her work and the hours passed quickly. Soon it was time to drive to the airport and meet Mrs. Bretton's plane.

She wondered how she would recognize her grandmother and what she would say to her first. There were so many things to tell and so many questions to ask.

As it happened, it was Alice Bretton who recognized Shay. A tiny, Helen Hayes-type, with snow-white hair done up in a bun and quick, sparkling eyes, Mrs. Bretton came right up to her granddaughter and said, "Why, dear, you look just like Robert!"

Shay was inordinately glad that she resembled someone; Lord knew, she looked nothing like Rosamond and never had. It was that gladness that broke the ice and allowed her to hug the small woman standing before her. "I'm so happy to see you," she said, and then she had to laugh because, looking down through a mist of tears, she could see that Alice was wearing bowling shoes with her trim, tasteful suit.

"They're so comfortable, don't you know!" Alice cried in good-natured self-defense.

Shay looked forward to telling Mitch that Mrs. Bretton did indeed wear bowling shoes, though she obviously wasn't a bag lady and it was doubtful that she had bunions.

Talking with her grandmother proved remarkably easy, considering all the years and all the heartaches that might have separated them. The two women chattered nonstop all the way back to Skyler Beach, Shay asking questions, Alice answering them.

Shay's eyes were hazel because hazel eyes ran in the Bretton family, she was told, and yes, Robert had wanted to marry Rosamond, but she'd refused. He had tried to see Shay many times, but she had always been away in some school, out of his reach. Rosamond had never allowed any of his letters or phone calls to Shay to get through.

Alice patted her sensible, high-quality purse. "But I have most of those letters right here. When they came back, Robert saved them."

Shay worked at keeping her mind on her driving, and it was hard. She wanted to pull over to the side of the freeway and read all of her father's letters, one after another. "Why didn't Rosamond want him to see me or even talk to me?"

Alice sighed, and if she bore Rosamond Dallas any ill-will, it wasn't visible in the sweet lines of her face. "Lord only knows. She wasn't very happy as a child, you know, and I guess she didn't want anything to do with anyone from Springfield. Not even her own baby's father."

Rosamond had said very little about her life in Springfield, only that her mother drank too much and her father, a railroad worker, had died in an accident when she was four years old. "Did you know Rosamond as a girl?"

Alice shook her head. "I only met her after she'd started to date Robert. She was beautiful, but I—well,

I had my misgivings about her. She was rather wild, you know.''

Shay could imagine her mother as a young girl, looking for approbation and love even in those pre-fame days. It was strange that the search had never stopped, that Rosamond had gone from man to man all her life. "I wish I'd known about you and about my father.''

Alice reached across the car seat to pat Shay's knee. "You'll know me, and I've brought along things to help you know your father, too.'' Suddenly the elderly woman looked alarmed. "I do hope I'm not keeping you from your work, dear!''

Shay thought of the commercials and the irate customers and the stacks of contracts and factory invoices she had left behind at Reese Motors. "My work will definitely keep until tomorrow. You can stay for a while, can't you?''

"Oh, yes. Nobody waiting at home but my parakeet, my cat and my bridge club. Now tell me all about this boy of yours. Hank, isn't it? You know, it's a funny thing, but your great-grandfather's name was Henry and they called him Hank, don't you know...''

Chapter Ten

Shay bit her lower lip as the ringing began on the other end of the line. It was just plain unconscionable to awaken someone at that hour of the night, but after reading her father's gentle, innocuous letters, she felt a deep need to touch base.

On the third ring, Mitch answered with an unintelligible grumble.

"She wears bowling shoes," Shay said.

"You woke me up to tell me that?" He didn't sound angry, just baffled.

"I thought you'd want to know." She paused, drew a deep breath. "Oh, Mitch, Alice is a wonderful woman."

"She's your grandmother. What else could she be besides wonderful?"

"Flatterer."

"You love it."

I love you, Shay thought. "Good night, Mitch," she said.

He laughed, a wonderful rumbling, sleepy sound. "Good night, princess."

Shay was glad that no one could see her, there in the darkness of her kitchen. She kissed the telephone receiver before she put it back in place.

Alice was still sleeping the next morning when Shay left for work. Rather than disturb her grandmother, she scribbled a note that included her office telephone number and crept out. Alice had made it very clear, the night before, that she didn't want to disrupt Shay's life in any way.

On the way to Reese Motors, Shay marveled that life could follow the same dull and rocky road for so many years, and then suddenly take a series of crazy turns. She'd met Mitch, she'd found her grandmother, she was about to start the business she had only dreamed of—and all this had taken place in a period of a few weeks.

When Shay arrived at work, she found Richard waiting in her office with the fourth and final storyboard. She was relieved; after this, she would never have to make a fool of herself on camera again.

"It's a giant, hairy hand," Richard said with amazing enthusiasm.

"I can see that, Richard," Shay replied dryly, frowning at the storyboard. "When are we filming this one?"

"Tomorrow, I hope. We had to special order that hand, you know."

Shay sighed inwardly. "It won't collapse or anything, will it?"

"Absolutely not. Would I risk your life that way?"

Shay shrugged philosophically. "I don't know, Richard. You almost smothered me in sugar the other day, so I thought I'd ask."

"Marvin's going to be pleased with these commercials, Shay," Richard said on an unexpectedly charitable note. "You've done a great job. The first spot aired late last night. You looked great, even in a bee suit."

Shay grinned, unable to resist saying, "I'll bet people are buzzing about it."

Richard laughed and left the office, taking the storyboard with him.

At noon, Alice arrived at Reese Motors by taxi, all dressed up for the lunch date she and Shay had made the night before. Shay proudly introduced her to Ivy, all the salesmen and even the mechanics in the repair section.

"I saw you on television today, dear," the elderly woman announced moderately over a chef's salad. "You were dressed as a bee, of all things." Alice looked puzzled, as though she thought Shay might say she was mistaken.

Briefly, Shay explained about Marvin's penchant for creative advertising.

"We have a car dealer like that in Springfield," Alice said seriously, and there was an endearing look of bafflement in her eyes. "He let a mouthful of water run down his chin and said he was liquidating last year's models."

"Oh, Lord," Shay groaned. "Do me a favor and don't mention that around Reese Motors. Marvin would probably get wind of it and come up with some version of his own."

"Is there a young man in your life, dear?"

The abrupt change in subject matter caught Shay off guard. "I—well—yes, sort of—"

Alice smiled. "Good. They're not all wasters like that Eliott person, you know."

Shay wondered what Alice would think of Mitch if she knew how he had hijacked her granddaughter to a private beach and made love to her in the sand. The memory of her own responses brought throbbing color to Shay's cheeks.

"What is his name, dear? What does he do?"

"His name is Mitch Prescott. He's the man who found you for me," Shay said, somewhat hesitantly.

Alice did not pursue the matter. "My, but you do look like your father," she said in a faraway voice.

That evening, after work, Shay drove to the Victorian house she hoped to restore and parked at the curb. The place was derelict, and yet, in her mind's eye, she could see so many possibilities for it. Suddenly she wanted that disreputable old white elephant with a consuming ache.

She drove home to find Alice happily cooking dinner and Mitch helping. The way the two of them were chattering, they might have known each other for ten years instead of ten minutes. It was crazy, but Shay was just a little jealous of both of them.

"Sit down, dear, sit down," Alice ordered, gesturing toward a chair at the kitchen table. "You look all worn out."

Over Alice's neatly coiffed and blue-rinsed head, Mitch gave Shay an evil wink.

Shay sighed and sat down, grateful for the coffee that was immediately set before her. "You two are going to spoil me if you keep this up. What will I do without you?"

The question, so innocently presented, caused a stiff silence. Mitch gazed off through the window over the sink, but Alice recovered quickly. "I was just telling your young man that I might sell my house and move out here for good. I could get a little apartment, don't you know."

Shay's eyes widened. "You would do that? You would actually move here, just to be near Hank and me?"

"You're my family," Alice said softly. "All I have in the world. Of course I'd move to be near you. That's if you'd want—if I wouldn't be in the way—"

"Never." Shay rose from her chair and embraced this woman who had come to mean so much to her in such a short time. "You could never be in the way."

"Our Mr. Prescott might have a thing or two to say about that," Alice pointed out with a misty wryness as she and Shay drew apart. "He has plans for you, you know."

Mitch was no longer looking out the window, and a grin tilted one side of his mouth and lit his eyes. His entire demeanor said that he did indeed have plans for Shay, and none of them could be mentioned in front of her grandmother.

Shay waited until Alice wasn't looking and gave Mitch a slow, saucy wink.

Color surged up from the neck of his dark blue T-shirt and he tossed Shay a mock scowl in return. "Actually," he said, "I think Shay needs a grandmother around to keep her in line. I've tried, but the job is too big for me."

Alice chuckled and gave him a slight shove. "Step aside, handsome," she said. "I've got to get these biscuits in the oven or they won't be ready in time for supper."

Mitch caught Shay by the hand as he passed her, pulling her out of her chair and into the living room, where he promptly drew her close and kissed her. It was a thorough kiss that left Shay unsteady on her feet and just a bit flushed in the face.

Holding her close, Mitch whispered against the bridge of her nose, "If your grandmother wasn't in the next room, lady..."

Shay trembled with the delicious feeling of wanting him. In a low, teasing voice, she retorted, "You shameless rascal, how can you say such a thing when you've been flirting with another woman under my very nose?"

Mitch grinned. "What can I say? I took one look at Alice and I was smitten."

"Smitten?"

He pulled her toward the couch, sat down, positioned her on his lap. His hand moved beneath her skirt to stroke her thigh. "Smitten," he confirmed.

Shay's breath had quickened and her blood felt warm enough to melt her veins. She slapped away his hand and it returned, unerringly, to create sweet havoc on the flesh of her upper leg.

"So," he said, as though he weren't driving her wild with the brazen motion of his fingers. "Have you decided whether or not to take the house Todd showed you?"

Shay could barely breathe. "I'm...waiting for... estimates."

"I see."

Again, Shay removed his hand; again it returned. "Rat," she muttered.

Alice was humming in the kitchen, happy in her work, probably pleased with herself for giving the young lovers some time alone. Mitch continued to caress Shay, slowly, rhythmically, skillfully.

She buried her mouth in the warmth of his neck to muffle the soft moan his attentions forced her to utter.

"You look a bit flushed, dear," Alice commented, minutes later, over a dinner of chicken, green beans and biscuits, her gentle eyes revealing worry. "I hope you aren't coming down with something."

"She's perfectly healthy," Mitch replied with an air of authority.

Beneath the surface of the table, Shay's foot moved and her heel made solid contact with Mitch's shin. He didn't even flinch.

After dinner, he and Shay did the dishes together while Alice rested on Hank's bed. She'd closed the door behind her, but Shay still felt compelled to keep her voice down.

"If you ever do a thing like that again, Mitch Prescott..."

He wrapped the dishtowel around Shay's waist, turned slightly and pulled her against him. "You can be sure that I'll do it again," he muttered. "And you'll react just the same way."

Shay knew that he was right and flushed, furious that he had such power over her and yet glad of it, too. Her body was still reverberating with the force of her response to those stolen moments of pleasure. "You are vain and arrogant!" she whispered.

He put one hand inside her blouse to cup her breast, his thumb moving her bra out of place and then caressing her nipple. "I'm going to forget that copy of my manuscript when I leave here tonight," he said, his lips barely touching Shay's. "You, of course, will throw up your hands in dismay and tell your grandmother that you've got to return it to me immediately."

Shay shuddered with desire, still held close to solid proof of his masculinity by the dishtowel. His fingers were plucking gently at her nipple and she couldn't reason, let alone argue. "B-bastard," she said, and that was the extent of her rebellion.

Mitch slid the top of her blouse aside and bent his head to taste her now-throbbing nipple with an utterly brazen lack of haste. In fact, he satisfied himself at leisure before tugging her bra back into place and straightening her blouse. And then he left.

Shay finished the dishes and then, hating herself, tapped at the door of Hank's room. "Alice?"

The answer was a sleepy, "Yes, dear?"

"Mitch forgot something here, and I've got to take it to him. I'll be back soon."

Two hours later Shay returned, hair and clothes slightly rumpled, lips swollen with Mitch's kisses. Alice was knitting, the television tuned to a mystery program, and even in the dim light of the living room, Shay could see the sparkle in her grandmother's eyes. The lady was clearly nobody's fool.

"Did you have a nice time, dear?"

Every part of Shay was pulsing with the "nice time" she'd had in Mitch Prescott's arms. "Yes," she said, in classic understatement, and then she excused herself to take a bath and get ready for bed.

Because the last commercial was being taped the next morning and Alice wanted to watch, Shay arrived at work with her grandmother in tow.

The enormous hairy hand towered in the middle of the main showroom, and Shay shook her head as she looked at it. She was given a flowing white dress to put on in the rest room, and Richard's assistant applied her makeup.

At least the showroom had been closed for whatever length of time it would take to get the spot on video-tape, Shay noted with relief. Using a stepladder, she climbed into the palm of that hand and stretched out on her side, trying to keep the dress from riding up. Richard followed her up and carefully closed the huge fingers of the hand around her.

Before going back down the stepladder he winked at Shay and told her again that Marvin was going to be proud of her.

"This is really the way Faye Raye got her start, huh?" Shay muttered, trying to be a good sport about the whole thing. After all, this was the last commercial she would ever appear in.

Looking down, Shay saw her grandmother talking with Ivy, but there was no sign of Mitch. Her feelings about that were mixed. On the one hand, she hated to have him see her in such a ridiculous position. On the other, it was always comforting to know that he was there somewhere.

This time the cameras were above her, on the mezzanine, along with an enormous fan. A microphone had been hidden in the neckline of Shay's chiffon dress.

"Ready?" Richard called from his place between the two cameramen.

Shay nodded; she was as ready as she was ever going to get.

The fan started up and Shay's dress and hair moved in the flow of air. She practiced her smile and mentally rehearsed her line as the cameras panned over the selection of cars available in the showroom. When she saw them swing in her direction, she beamed, even though the fan was buffeting the air from her lungs, and gasped, "You'll go ape when you see the deals we're making at Reese Motors! Come on down and talk to us at 6832 Discount Way, right here in Skyler Beach!"

"Perfect!" Richard exulted, and Shay's relief was such that for a moment she sank into the hollow of that giant ape hand and closed her eyes. One of the salesmen came to help her out from under the hairy fingers and down the ladder.

"You were magnificent!" Alice said when Shay came to stand before her, but there was an expression of profound relief in her eyes.

"I'm just glad it's over," Shay answered, wondering if Alice would tell her friends back home that her granddaughter earned her living by dressing up as a bee or lying in a huge and hairy hand.

"Well," Alice announced brightly, "I'm off to look at apartments with Ivy's young man. I may be late, so I took the liberty of setting out one of the casseroles you had in your freezer." The older woman's eyes shifted from Shay to Ivy, and they sparkled with pride. "My granddaughter is a very organized young woman, don't you know. She'll make a fine caterer."

The vote of confidence uplifted Shay; she said goodbye to Alice and went into the rest room to put on her normal clothes and redo her makeup. Within twenty minutes, she was so involved in her work that she'd forgotten all about her brief stint as the captive of a mythical ape.

After work, Shay met briefly with one of the contractors providing an estimate on the renovation of the old house. His bid was higher than the one Todd had gotten, but she reviewed it carefully anyway.

Over the next three days, the rest of the estimates came in, straggle fashion. Shay looked them all over and decided to go with Todd's original choices all the way down the line. She called her friend and, after taking one deep breath, told him that she would lease the house he'd shown her if the option to buy later still stood.

"You're certainly efficient, Todd," she said after the details had been discussed. "Alice loves that apartment you found for her. She's looking forward to becoming a 'beach bunny,' as she put it."

Todd laughed. "She's something else, isn't she? I'm glad you and Alice found each other, Shay."

Shay was glad, too, of course, for her own sake and for Hank's. What a surprise Alice would be to him when he came home from his trip! Even before her illness, Rosamond had never been very interested in the child, but now he would have someone besides Shay to claim as family.

For all these good things that were happening, there was one dark spot on Shay's horizon. "H-have you talked to Mitch in the last few days?"

There was intuitive understanding in Todd's voice as he replied, "He's working like a madman, Shay. I think he's got another project lined up for when he's done with Rosamond's book, and he's anxious to get to it."

Another project. Shay thought of Mitch's earlier books—she'd skimmed through all four of them during the past few days—and she was alarmed. Good God, did he mean to tangle with the Mafia again? With drug dealers and Nazis and militant members of the Klan? He'd be killed!

She said goodbye in the most moderate voice she could manage, then hung up the telephone with a bang and rushed out of her office, past Ivy's empty desk, through the deserted showroom downstairs and across the parking lot to her car.

Ten minutes later she was knocking on Mitch Prescott's front door.

His housekeeper, Mrs. Carraway, answered. "Hello, Mrs. Kendall," she said warmly. She probably knew a great deal about Shay's relationship with her employer, but Shay couldn't take the time to consider all the embarrassing ramifications of that now.

"Is Mr. Prescott at home? I really must see him as soon as possible."

Mrs. Carraway looked surprised. "Why, no, Mrs. Kendall. He's away on a research project or some such. I don't expect him back for nearly a week."

A week! Mitch was going to be gone for a whole week and he hadn't even bothered to say goodbye. Shay was devastated and she was angry and she was afraid. So afraid. Had he gone back to the jungles of Colombia, or perhaps to Beirut or Belfast or some other dangerous place? She swallowed her pride.

"Do you know if Mr. Prescott has left the United States?"

The housekeeper's face revealed something Shay found even harder to bear than surprise, and that was sympathy. "I really don't know, Mrs. Kendall. I'm sorry."

Shay muttered something polite and quite insensible and turned away. She should have known better than to get involved with a man who lived his life in the fast lane, she thought fiercely. She should have known better.

When Shay arrived home she found her grandmother packed to leave for Springfield on an early morning plane. Alice was eager to tie up the loose ends of her life in Missouri and get back to Skyler Beach.

Shay didn't want her to go, even for such a short time. Everyone she loved, it seemed, was either away or about to leave. "If you'd stay just a few more days, you could meet Hank—"

Alice left her packing to kiss Shay's cheek. "I'll be back soon, don't you worry. Besides, the boy will need his room."

"It isn't going to be the same without you," Shay said as Alice went back to the two suitcases propped on the living room sofa to arrange and rearrange their contents.

Alice went on working, but there was gentle understanding in the look she passed to Shay. "You think I'm going to get back there and change my mind, don't you?"

Shay sank into the easy chair nearest the couch. "Your friends are there. Your house, your memories."

The old woman gestured toward the stack of photo albums she'd brought with her. They constituted a loving chronicle of Robert Bretton's life, virtually from birth. "My memories are in my mind and my heart and in those albums over there. And my future is right here, in Skyler Beach. In fact, I'm thinking seriously of renting one of the shops in your building and opening a little yarn shop. I've always wanted to do something like that."

Shay reached out and took one of the albums from the coffee table, opening it on her lap. Lord knew, she'd studied them all so many times that every last picture was permanently imprinted in her mind, but seeing her father's face, so like her own, was a comfort. "A yarn shop?" she echoed, not really absorbing what Alice had said.

"Robert's father provided very well for me," Alice reflected, "and I've got no worries where money is concerned." She closed the suitcases and their fastenings clicked into place one by one. "In my time, very few women had their own businesses, but I always dreamed of it."

Shay looked up and closed the album. "You could teach knitting classes, as well as sell yarn," she speculated, getting into the spirit of things.

Alice nodded. "I've arranged for Ivy to come and pick me up, Shay. She's driving me to a hotel near the airport."

Shay set the album aside, stung. "I would have been glad to—"

"I know, dear. I know. You would have been glad to drive me to the airport tomorrow at the crack of dawn and interrupt your entire day, but I won't let you do it."

"But—"

"No buts. My mind is made up. You've been running yourself ragged, what with our talks about your father and your job and those silly commercials, not to mention the catering service. I want you to eat a good supper, take a nice bath and go to bed early."

Shay couldn't help smiling, though she felt sad. Mitch was gone, Hank was gone, and now Alice was going, too. "Spoken like a true grandmother. Won't you at least let me drive you to your hotel?"

"Absolutely not. Ivy and her young man are taking me and that's final." Alice lowered her voice and bent toward Shay, her eyes sparkling. "I do believe they're planning a rather romantic evening; though, of course, I'll never know."

Shay laughed and shook her head, but inside she wished that she were looking forward to just such an evening with Mitch.

The call came within minutes of Alice's departure with Todd and Ivy. There would be no quiet dinner, no comforting bath, no going to bed early. Rosamond had taken an abrupt turn for the worse, the doctor told Shay, and the diagnosis was pneumonia. Rosamond was being taken by ambulance to the nearest hospital.

Shay raced to Skyler Beach's only hospital, driving so recklessly that it was a miracle she didn't have an accident and end up in the intensive care unit with her mother.

Rosamond had arrived several minutes before her daughter, but it was some time before Shay was permitted to see her. She looked small and incredibly emaciated, Rosamond did, lying there beneath an oxygen tent, and there were so many tubes and monitoring devices that it was difficult to get close to her.

Shay had expected this to happen, but now, standing beside her mother's hospital bed, she found that expecting something and being prepared for it are two very different things. She wept silently as she kept her vigil and, toward morning, when Rosamond passed away, there were no more tears to cry.

Shay walked out of the hospital room, down the hallway, into the elevator. She drove home in a stupor—there was a storm gathering in the sky—and somehow gathered the impetus to dial the telephone number Garrett had left for her. The first person to learn of Rosamond's death, besides Shay herself, had to be Riley.

After talking to a housekeeper and then a secretary, Shay was finally put through to Garrett, who told her that Hank and Riley were on another part of the ranch, participating in a roundup.

As the storm outside broke, flinging the rain and the wind at the walls of her tiny house, Shay sank onto her sofa, the telephone balanced on her knees. "Garrett, it's Rosamond. She—she—"

Garrett waited, probably guessing what was coming, for Shay to go on.

"She died early this morning. Pneumonia. Will you tell Riley for me?"

"Of course," Garrett answered gently. "I'm sorry, Amazon. I'm really sorry. Have any arrangements been made?"

"Not yet. I just—" Shay paused, pushing rain-dampened hair back from her forehead. She didn't remember getting wet. "I just got home."

"Are you all right?"

"I think so."

"Call someone. You shouldn't be alone."

No, I shouldn't, Shay thought without any particular emotion, but I am. "I think I'll be all right. You'll—you'll bring Hank home right away?"

"Right away, sweetheart. Hang tough; we're as good as on the road right now."

Shay mumbled a goodbye and hung up the telephone. Then she got up and made her way into her room. Clydesdale, her carousel horse, stood in one corner, his head high, his painted mane flowing.

Shay rested her forehead against his neck and this time she wept for all the happiness that might have been.

Chapter Eleven

Of all Rosamond's husbands, only Riley came to the funeral. A tall man with rough-hewn features and a deep melodic voice that echoed in the hearts of his hearers, he seemed, after all those years of fame, perpetually baffled by the attention paid him. Looking uncomfortable in his dark suit, he delivered a simple and touching eulogy to the remarkably small gathering. It seemed apt that the sky was dark and heavy with an impending storm.

Ivy and Todd were there to offer moral support, though neither of them had really known Rosamond at all. Marvin and Jeannie Reese, recently returned from their trip and still showing signs of jet lag, were present, too, also for Shay's sake. That left Riley, Garrett and Shay herself as true mourners. Garrett's wife, Maggie, was looking after the children.

It wasn't much of a turnout, Shay thought, looking around her. Rosamond had made such a mark on the world, but it appeared that she had touched few individual lives in any lasting way. There was a lesson in that, but Shay was too distracted to make sense of it at the moment.

She wished for Mitch with a poignancy that came from the depths of her and when she turned away from the graveside, he was there. He took both her hands in his.

"I just heard," he said hoarsely. "Shay, I'm sorry."

Shay nodded, her throat thick with tears that made speech impossible.

It began to rain and the mourners dispersed, carrying black umbrellas, their heads down. Shay stood in the open, facing Mitch, wanting nothing so much as to be held by him. He took her arm and led her toward his sleek blue car, parked behind the somber trio of limousines.

After settling her in the passenger seat and closing the door against the drizzling rain, he approached Riley and Garrett. Shay watched through the droplets of water beading on the windshield as he offered his hand, probably in introduction, and said something. The two other men nodded in reply and then Mitch came back to the car.

Shay didn't ask what he'd told them; in essence, she didn't care. "You're here," she remarked. That, for the moment, was enough.

Mitch patted her arm and started up the powerful car. "I'll always be here," he said, and then they were leaving the cemetery behind.

They were almost to Mitch's house when Shay came to her senses. "I should go home. Hank is there, and—"

"Hank is all right."

Shay knew that was true. Hank was safe with Maggie. He'd barely known Rosamond anyway; her death had little meaning to him except as something that had upset his mother. "I didn't expect to grieve, you know," she said in a small voice. "Rosamond and I weren't close."

Mitch was concentrating on the sharp turn onto his property. "She was your mother," he answered, as though that made sense of everything. And in a way, Shay supposed, it did.

The rain was beating down by the time Mitch stopped the car in the driveway, and Mrs. Carraway stood holding the front door open as they dashed toward the house.

"I've made dinner," the housekeeper said in the entryway as Mitch began peeling Shay's sodden suit jacket from her shoulders. "I'll go home now, if that's all right."

"Be careful," Mitch said, without looking at the woman. "It's nasty out there."

Mrs. Carraway hesitated. "Mrs. Kendall?" she said, her eyes steady on Shay's face though it was clear that she would rather have looked away. "I'm truly sorry about your mother."

"Thank you," Shay answered. Her teeth began to chatter and she hugged herself, trying to get warm.

Mrs. Carraway went out and Mitch lifted Shay into his arms and carried her up the stairs and into his bedroom. The hot tub had been filled and the water steamed invitingly.

Mitch set Shay on her feet and, after flipping a switch that made the water in the tub churn and bubble, he gently removed the rest of her clothes. Then he lowered her into the wondrously warm, welcoming water.

Shay shuddered violently as her cold-numbed body adjusted itself to the change of temperature. "F-feels go-good," she said.

Mitch sat on his heels beside the tub and reached out to touch her hair. "You look like a lady in need of a glass of brandy and a good meal. Are you hungry?"

Shay felt guilty surprise. "Yes," she marveled. "That's awful, isn't it?"

"Awful? I don't follow your logic, princess." His hand lingered in her hair, and it felt as good to her as the surging warmth of the hot tub.

"I just left my mother's funeral. I shouldn't be here."

Mitch shook his head in exasperation, but his eyes were gentle and so was his voice. "Next you'll be asking for a hair shirt. You belong here, with me. Especially now."

"But Hank—"

"If you want Hank, I'll go and get him."

Shay bit her lower lip. "You'd do that?"

"Of course I would."

"I—I'd like to call him later, to make sure he's okay."

"Fine." Mitch bent, kissed her forehead and then left the room. He returned several minutes later carrying a tray of food, two crystal snifters and a bottle of brandy.

Shay ate without leaving the hot tub and then slid the tray away. Mitch was sitting on the tiled edge, wearing a blue terry-cloth bathrobe and dangling his hairy legs in the water.

Having finished her dinner and a hefty dose of brandy, the warm water soothing her further, Shay began to yawn. With a tender light in his dark eyes, Mitch helped her from the tub, dried her gently with a soft towel and bundled her into a bathrobe much like the one he was wearing. That done, he guided Shay to the bed and tucked her in.

He kissed her forehead and then turned away. Shay watched, half-awake, as he shed his blue bathrobe and flung it back toward the bed, just missing the target, and then lowered himself into the hot tub, his tanned and muscled body hidden from view.

Shay was disappointed. "Did you know that you're beautiful?" she yawned.

Mitch chuckled and braced himself against the edge of the tub, his arms folded on the tiles, his brandy glass in one hand. "Am I?"

"Ummm-hmmm."

"Sleep, princess."

Shay stretched, warm in Mitch's bathrobe and his bed, her mind floating. "I wished for you . . . and you were there . . . just like a prince in a fairy tale. You won't . . . you won't leave me, will you?"

"I won't leave you." The words were gruff, and they seemed to come from a great distance. "Go to sleep, my love."

"Come here. Hold me."

She heard a splashing sound as Mitch got out of the hot tub, and watched as he dried himself with a huge green towel. And then he was there, beside her, strong and warm, his flesh a hard wall that kept the rest of the world at bay.

They slept for a long time, and then awakened simultaneously to make love. The world was dark and the only sound Shay could hear, besides her own breathing and Mitch's, was the bubbling of the hot tub.

She crooned and stretched in luxurious abandon as he kissed and tongued her breasts and her stomach, stroked her with his hands. Shay was seized by a keening tension as Mitch loved her and she clasped his shoulders in her hands. "Now, now," she breathed.

He parted her legs with a motion of one knee and took her in one swift, masterful stroke, filling her with himself, driving out all thoughts of death and sadness and loss.

With a cry, Shay arched against him, her body acting on its own, clutching at life, affirming life, demanding life. "Oh, God," she gasped, breathless. "Mitch, Mitch—"

He fit his hands beneath her quivering bottom and lifted her up, to possess her more fully, to be possessed by her. "It's all right," he said to that part of Shay that was ashamed to feel such primitive need. There were no words, however, as their bodies waged their tender and furious battle, rising and falling in a feverish search for fulfillment that ended in a hoarse shout for Mitch and a sob for Shay.

He held her, his chest heaving and damp beneath her cheek, as she cried.

"How could I—how could I do that? My mother—"

Mitch's hand smoothed her hair back from her face and then his arm tightened around her. "Shhh. You're alive, Shay. Your body was reminding you of that; it's an instinctive thing, so stop tormenting yourself."

"You're just trying to make me feel better!"

"Of course I am, I love you. But what I said was true, nevertheless. Any brush with death, direct or indirect, will produce that response in a healthy person."

He spoke with such authority. Shay thought of Mitch's encounters with death, all chronicled so forthrightly in his books, and wondered whom he'd been with afterward. Some Colombian señorita? "That lady pilot, in Chapter Six of *The Connection*—"

Mitch gave an exaggerated snore.

Shay jabbed him in the ribs and then, conversely, cuddled even closer. She fell asleep and dreamed that she and Mitch were making love on the lush floor of a Colombian jungle, vines and tropical plants and enormous, colorful flowers making a canopy for their bed.

Life went on, Shay discovered, and it carried her with it. She said goodbye to Riley and Garrett and Maggie, got Hank into school and gave two weeks' notice at her job.

"We'll be sorry to see you go," Marvin said quietly, sitting behind his broad, paper-littered desk. "But Jeannie and I both wish you the best of luck wth your business."

Shay let out a sigh of relief. Marvin was a reasonable man, but she had been worried that he'd think her ungrateful. "Thank you."

Behind his fashionable wire glasses, Marvin's eyes twinkled. "Those commercials you made were first-rate, Shay. I couldn't have done a better job myself."

Shay grinned. "It'll be years before I live those spots down," she answered. "Yesterday, in the supermarket, a little girl recognized me as the bee and called her mother over to meet me. It was half an hour before I could get back to my shopping. To make matters worse, Hank is selling my autograph for twenty-five cents a shot."

Marvin sat back in his chair, chuckling. His checkered jacket appeared capable of leaping into the conversation on its own, and Shay blinked as he replied,

"Twenty-five cents, huh? That's definitely the big time."

Shay sighed philosophically. "Not really. He gets two-fifty for Riley's signature. The poor man must have written his name a hundred times while he was with Hank, just to keep the kid in spending money."

"Enterprising boy, that Hank," Marvin said with quiet pride. "Takes after his mother."

"That's a compliment, I hope."

"Absolutely. If you need help of any kind, Shay, you come to Jeannie and me."

Shay nodded and looked away, to hide the sudden tears that sprang to her eyes. "I'd better get back to work," she said softly, turning to go and then pausing at the door. "About my replacement—"

"I think Ivy can handle the job, don't you?"

Shay was delighted. She'd planned to suggest Ivy, but Marvin had saved her the trouble. "Yes."

"Get a new receptionist, then," Marvin said brusquely, tackling his paperwork with a flourish meant to hide emotions of his own. "Do it right away. Ivy will need to concentrate on learning your job and I want the transition to be made as smoothly as possible."

Shay saluted briskly, her lips twitching, and hurried out. Ivy was standing up at her computer terminal, at hopeful attention.

"The job is yours," Shay whispered.

"Ya-hoo!" Ivy shrieked.

Shay had obviously painted part of the old house herself, in a very light shade of blue and a pristine white. Both colors were well represented not only on the front of her coveralls but on her chin and her nose, too.

Watching her, Mitch ached with the love of her, the need of her.

He'd been hard at work on Rosamond's book for several weeks and now it was done, ready for Shay's final approval. He cleared his throat and she lifted her eyes to his face, her conversation with a similarly clad Alice falling off in midsentence.

"Mitch," she said.

Alice rubbed her hands down the legs of her tiny coveralls and did a disappearing act.

"The book?" Shay whispered.

Mitch extended a fat manila envelope. "Here it is, princess. Photo layouts and all."

She approached him, took the envelope, but her wide eyes never left his face. "I'll read it tonight," she said.

"I've missed you," he replied.

"We've both been busy." Her eyes were averted now. "Y-you're starting a new book, aren't you?"

Mitch sighed. The Alan Roget project was something they hadn't discussed. "I've gathered some material, yes."

She paled. "I—I guess I'd better get back to work," she said.

Something in her manner panicked Mitch. He wanted to shout at her, grasp her arm, anything. Instead he simply said her name.

Shay turned away from him, holding the manuscript in both arms. "It's over now, I guess," she said distractedly. "You have your life and I have mine."

"Over?" Mitch was stunned. He reached out then and caught her arm in one hand and wrenched her around to face him. "What the hell are you talking about?"

"W-we'll both be so busy now—"

"Busy?"

There were tears gathering along her eyelashes and her lower lip was quivering. "Shall I call you if there are any changes to be made? In—in the book, I mean?"

Mitch looked around him then, at the beautifully restored walls and ceilings, and suddenly he thought he understood what was happening. He'd served his purpose and now there was no place in Shay's life for him. "Yeah," he bit out, letting go of her arm. "You do that." He turned and walked out, not daring to look back.

Shay sat down on the newspaper-covered floor and opened the packet containing Mitch's manuscript. She had to rub her eyes several times before the typewritten words would come into focus.

"Where's Mitch?" Alice asked innocently, holding out a cup of coffee to Shay and sipping at one of her own.

Shay felt hollow and broken. "He's gone."

Alice manuevered herself into a cross-legged position on the floor, facing her granddaughter. "Gone? I don't like the sound of that, Shay. It has a permanent ring."

"It is permanent," Shay confirmed sadly.

"Are you mad?" Alice asked in a low incredulous tone. "That man loves you, Shay, and you love him!"

"You don't understand. H-he's writing another book."

By now, Alice was a member of the necessarily small group of people who knew that Mitch Prescott and the mysterious "Zebulon" were one and the same person. She had read his books avidly, one after another, Shay knew, so she should have gotten the point. It was obvious from what she said next she hadn't. "Isn't that what writers do? Finish one book and start another?"

Shay was suddenly annoyed, and the sharpness of her tone reflected that, as did the hot color in her cheeks. "It isn't the writing that bothers me! It's the research! Alice, he could be killed, captured, tortured!"

"That's why you're throwing him over? Shay, I thought you were made of better stuff."

Alice's words, though moderately spoken, stung Shay. "I'd be sweating blood every time he left the house, Alice! I love him too much to—"

"On the contrary, dear," Alice broke in quietly. "It seems to me that you don't love him enough."

Shay leaped to her feet, insulted, and stomped out of the room, out of the house. Alice could get back to her apartment on her own, she knew; she had bought a small car from Marvin Reese and was already an expert at navigating every part of Skyler Beach. Shay got into her own car and drove away, going far too fast.

She got a speeding ticket before she had traveled four blocks, and the fact that she deserved it did nothing to temper her mood. By the time she got back to her house, she was a wreck.

When Hank came home from school, he took one look at his mother and asked if he could go over to his friend Louie's house to play until dinner. Feeling guilty, Shay smiled and ruffled his hair. "Have you got any homework?"

"They don't give homework in the first grade, Mom," he said indulgently.

"Oh."

Hank was perched on the arm of her chair, his eyes taking in the paint smudges on her face, her tangled hair, the coveralls. "Do you like your new job, Mom?"

"I haven't started it yet, but I'm sure I'll like it a lot."

"Will you have to dress like that?"

Shay laughed. "No. I painted my office today, that's all."

"I thought the contractors were supposed to do all that stuff."

"I wanted to do my office myself. And don't ask me why, tiger, because I don't know."

"Are we going to live over there, where your office is, I mean?"

Shay shook her head. "There won't be room, once all the other shops open. I rented the last one today."

"You didn't rent Grammie's knit shop out, did you?" Hank demanded. Rosamond had always been Rosamond to him, but Alice, who had won his affections instantly, was "Grammie."

"Of course I didn't," Shay said with a frown. "What made you ask a thing like that?"

Hank's thin shoulders moved in a shrug. "I was just wondering."

Shay didn't believe him. Somehow, in the uncanny way of a child, he'd sensed that she and Alice had had words. She felt ashamed of her outburst now and made a mental note to call Alice and apologize the moment Hank went outside to play. "Grammie's looking forward to having you help her at the shop."

Hank looked manfully apologetic. "I won't be able to go every day. I've got little-league practice and stuff like that."

"I'm sure Grammie will understand."

"And the guys might tease me if they see me messing around with yarn and junk."

Shay kept a straight face. "They might."

Hank brightened. "I'd better go and find Louie now. See ya."

"You be back here in half an hour, buddy," Shay warned. "Supper will be ready then."

"Okay, Mom," he called, the sound mingling with the slamming of the front door.

Shay got out of her chair, took a quick shower and put on her bathrobe and slippers. This was a night to be dissolute, she decided as she put hot dogs on to boil and opened a can of pork and beans to serve with them. After tearing the top off a bag of potato chips, she dialed Alice's number.

"I'm sorry," she said without preamble.

"Call Mitch Prescott and tell him the same thing," Alice immediately responded.

Shay stiffened. "I will not."

"You're a fool, then," Alice answered. "A man like that doesn't come around every few months, like quarterly taxes and the newest TV miniseries, you know."

"You're impossible!"

"Yes," Alice agreed. "But you love me."

Shay laughed in spite of herself. "That's true. I'll see you tomorrow, then?"

"Absolutely. My cash register and some of my yarn are supposed to be delivered."

Shay was hanging up the telephone just as Hank dashed in, flushed from some backyard game and ready for his supper. He ate and took his bath without complaint, then settled down to watch the one hour of television allowed him on a school night.

Shay settled into the easy chair in the living room and began reading Mitch's manuscript again. It was a great improvement over the first draft, which had been wonderful in its own right, and she again had the feeling that she was meeting Rosamond Dallas for the first time. She stopped long enough to see that Hank brushed his teeth and said his prayers, but the story of her mother's life drew her back.

She turned the last page at three-fourteen that morning, wide awake and awed by the quiet power of Mitch's writing. She had expected the book to need minor changes. But it was perfect as it was. Unfortunately. Revisions would have given her an excuse to work closely with Mitch again.

Stiff and sore, Shay set the manuscript carefully aside and rose from her chair. Working with Mitch would have been a foolish indulgence, considering her decision to end the relationship. No, it was better this way, she told herself—she would simply call him in the morning and tell him that she could see no problems with the book being published just as it was. Their association would then be officially ended, and Shay could go on with her life.

What kind of life was it going to be, without Mitch? The question chewed at Shay long after she'd fallen into bed. Sure, she had Hank and Alice and her business, but what was she going to do without those fevered bouts of lovemaking that always left her exhausted but strangely revitalized, too? What was she going to do without the laughter and the fights and the adventures?

Adventures. Shay sighed. That was the key word. She simply wasn't cut out to sit at home, chewing her fingernails, while the man she loved risked his life in order to research some new journalistic feat.

Alice's accusation came back to haunt her then, echoing in her mind. She did *too* love Mitch enough.

She loved him, as she had maintained to Alice, too much. If she married Mitch and then he was killed, she would be devastated.

She sat up in bed with a jolt. Only in that moment did it occur to her that she would be just as devastated if he died without ever marrying her, ever touching her again. Why had she thought that separating herself from Mitch would save him?

The next morning was splashed in the singular glory of early October and Shay drove slowly up the hill to Mitch's house. The distant sound of a hammer made her walk around back instead of ringing the doorbell.

Mitch was kneeling on the roof of the playhouse, half a dozen nails jutting from his mouth, his tanned chest and shoulders bared to the crisp bite of the weather. Shay stood watching him for a moment, her heart caught in her throat.

He stopped swinging the hammer to look at her, and there was no welcome, no tenderness, in his eyes. "Well," he said.

Shay was careful not to reveal how much his coolness hurt her. "If you have a minute, I'd like to talk."

He began to drive another nail into another tiny shingle. "I'm busy."

Shay was shaken to her core, but she stood her ground. "I came to return the manuscript, Mitch," she lied. In truth, the book had been an afterthought, an excuse.

He went on working. "Leave it with Mrs. Carraway," he said brusquely.

"You aren't going to let me apologize, are you?" Shay reddened, embarrassed and hurt and yet unable to turn and walk away.

"Apologize all you want. I'm through playing the game, Shay."

"The game? What game?"

Now, Mitch set the hammer aside, but he remained on the roof of the playhouse and his manner was no friendlier. "You know what I'm talking about, Shay. You come to me when you need comfort or a roll in the hay, and then you run away again."

"A roll in the—my God, that's crude!"

The broad, sun-browned shoulders moved in a shrug cold enough to chill Shay. "Maybe so, but it's the truth. You want the fun, but you're too cowardly to make a real commitment, aren't you? Well, get yourself another flunky."

"You said you loved me!"

A small shingle splintered under the force of a blow from Mitch's hammer. "I do," he said, without looking at Shay. "But I don't want to play house anymore. I need the real thing."

Baffled and as broken as that shingle Mitch had just destroyed, Shay turned and hurried away.

Chapter Twelve

If there was one thing Shay learned in the coming weeks, it was how little she knew about the catering business. She made all the standard mistakes and a few new ones to boot. By the end of October her confidence was sorely shaken.

Alice lifted the furry Halloween costume she was making for Hank to her mouth and bit off a thread with her teeth. While her grandmother sewed at the kitchen table, Shay was frantically mixing the ingredients for enough lasagne to feed fifty people.

"You expected starting your own company to be easy, Shay?"

Shay sighed as she wrapped another panful of lasagne and put it into the freezer. "Of course I didn't. But I have to admit that I expected a lack of business to be the problem, not a surplus. I have four wedding receptions and people are already calling about Thanksgiving. Who ever heard of having Thanksgiving dinner catered, for heaven's sake?''

Alice chuckled. ''The solution seems obvious. Hire some help.''

Shay leaned back against the counter in a rare moment of indolence. ''I hate to do that, Alice. If things slow down, I'd have to let people go.''

''You'll just have to make it clear from the beginning that the work could be temporary.''

''All right, fine. But how am I going to make the time to interview these people, let alone train them to cook?''

Alice let the costume rest in her lap. ''Dear, dear, you are frazzled. You simply call the junior college. They have a Displaced Homemaker program, you know. Ask them to send over a few prospects. I'll do the interviewing for you, if you'd like, right in my shop. If any seem promising, I'll send them on to you.''

''You're brilliant,'' Shay said, bending to plant a kiss on her grandmother's forehead. ''How in the world did I ever get along without you?''

Alice chuckled and went back to her sewing. ''What are you wearing to the Reeses' Halloween party?'' she asked over the whir of Shay's portable machine.

Shay was mixing tomato sauce to pour over a layer of ricotta cheese. ''I'm not going.''

The sewing machine stopped. ''Not going? But it's going to be marvelous, with everyone in costume....''

''I plan to drop off the food and then leave, Alice, and that's that.''

''You're no fun at all. Where's your spirit of adventure?''

Shay remembered a few of the ''adventures'' she'd had with Mitch Prescott and felt sad. ''I've never been the adventurous type. Besides, I don't have a costume."

"You've got that bee suit. Wear that."

"Wear it? When I've been all this time trying to live it down? No way. I'll stay home and greet the trick-or-treaters, thank you very much."

"Party pooper."

Shay laughed. "What are you going to wear, by the way?"

The sewing machine was going again. "I'm dressing up as a punk rocker," Alice answered placidly. "Cyndi Lauper will have nothing on me."

Shay shook her head. It seemed odd that her grandmother was so full of life and she herself could think of nothing but work. She should wear the bee suit for Halloween after all, she thought. It was a costume that suited a drone.

Mitch was tired from the flight and sick to his stomach. Meetings with unrepentant serial killers tended to have that effect on him.

Mrs. Carraway was busy carving an enormous pumpkin at the kitchen table. "Hello, Mr. Prescott," she said, beaming. "Welcome back." She started to get up and Mitch gestured for her to stay put.

The last thing he wanted was food. He rummaged through a cupboard until he found a bottle of Scotch and poured himself a generous helping. "What are you doing?" he asked, frowning at the pile of pumpkin pulp and seeds on the table.

Mrs. Carraway arched an eyebrow, either at his drink or his question; Mitch didn't know which and didn't care. "Why, I'm making a jack-o'-lantern; it's Halloween."

Mitch lifted his glass in a silent salute to the holiday. He needed a shower and a shave and about eighteen hours of sleep and he'd just spent two days talking to a man who was a whole hell of a lot scarier than your run-of-the-mill hobgoblin. "How fitting," he said.

The housekeeper gave him a curious look, probably thinking that she'd signed on with a reprobate. "Are you all right, Mr. Prescott?"

He thought of Shay and how badly he needed her to hold him in her arms and remind him of all the things that made life good and wholesome and right. "No," he answered, refilling his glass and starting toward the doorway. He paused. "The world can be a very ugly place, Mrs. Carraway. You see, for some people, every day is Halloween." He lifted the glass and took a burning gulp of Scotch. "The trouble is, they're bona fide ghouls and they don't wear costumes so that you can recognize them."

Mrs. Carraway looked really worried. "Won't you have something to eat, Mr. Prescott? It's almost suppertime."

"I may never eat again," Mitch answered, thinking of the things Alan Roget had confessed to him. He shook his head as he climbed the stairs, drink in hand. The tough journalist. He had walked out of that interview feeling as though he'd been exposed to some plague of the spirit and he'd been back in his hotel room all of five seconds before being violently ill.

Mitch entered his massive bedroom and it was empty, though specters of Shay were everywhere: lounging in the hot tub, kneeling on the bed, counting the extra toothbrushes he kept in the bathroom cabinet.

He drained the glass of Scotch and rubbed his eyes, tired to the very core of his being. "Shay," he said. "Shay."

Shay felt an intuitive pull toward Mitch's house; the sensation was so strong that it distracted her from the food she'd prepared for the Reeses' Halloween party. She hurried to finish packing the cheeseballs and puff pastries and then went into her office to dial the familiar number.

This is silly, she told herself as Mitch's phone began to ring.

"Prescott residence," Mrs. Carraway answered briskly.

Shay bit her lower lip. She should hang up. Calling Mitch was asking for rejection; he'd made his feelings perfectly clear that day when Shay had gone to him to apologize. "Th-this is Shay Kendall, Mrs. Carraway."

"Thank heaven," the housekeeper whispered, with a note of alarm in her voice that made Shay's backbone go rigid. "Oh, Mrs. Kendall, I have no right interfering like this—I'll probably be fired—but Mr. Prescott is in a terrible way."

"What do you mean? What's wrong?"

"He's been away on business for several days, and he just got home an hour or so ago. He said some very strange things, Mrs. Kendall, about every day being Halloween for some people."

Shay closed her eyes, thinking of the monsters that had populated Mitch's books. "Is he there now?"

Mrs. Carraway suddenly burst into tears. "Please come, Mrs. Kendall. Please. I don't know what to do!"

Shay looked down at her watch and bit her lower lip. She had to deliver the food to Jeannie and Marvin's town house, but after that the evening would be free. "I'll be there as soon as I can," she promised. "Don't worry. Everything will be all right."

Lofty words, Shay thought as she hung up the telephone in her office. Suppose everything wasn't all right? Suppose Mitch wouldn't even see her?

After loading the Reeses' hors d'oeuvres into her new station wagon, Shay went back inside her building to find Alice just closing up her yarn shop. "Something is wrong with Mitch," she told her grandmother bluntly. "I've got to go to him as soon as I deliver the Reeses' order. Hank is going trick-or-treating with his friend Louie at six, but if I'm late..."

Alice looked concerned. "Of course I'll look after him, my dear. You take all the time you need."

Shay kissed her grandmother's lovely crinkled cheek and hurried out to her car. She made the drive to Marvin and Jeannie's house in record time, and virtually shoved the boxes of carefully prepared cheeseballs and crab puffs and paté-spread crackers into the hands of a maid hired to serve that evening.

Everything within Shay was geared toward reaching Mitch at the soonest possible moment, but some niggling little instinct within argued that she needed a way to get past whatever defenses he might have erected against her. She stopped at her house for a few minutes and then went on to Mitch's.

Mrs. Carraway answered the doorbell almost before Shay had lowered her finger from the button. If Mitch's housekeeper was surprised to find a velveteen bee standing on the doorstep, she didn't show it.

"Upstairs," she whispered. "In his room."

Shay made her cumbersome way up the stairs. This was no time to try to hide the fact that she knew the way to Mitch Prescott's bedroom.

She tapped at the closed door.

"Go away!" Mitch bellowed from within. His voice was thick. Was he drunk?

Shay drew a deep breath and knocked again, harder this time.

There was muffled swearing and then the door swung open. "Dammit, I said—" Mitch's voice fell away and his haunted eyes took in Shay's bee suit with disbelief.

"Trick or treat?" she chimed.

"Good God," Mitch replied, but he stepped back so that Shay could enter the room.

She immediately pulled off the hood with its bobbing antennae and tossed it aside. After that, she struggled out of the rest of the suit, too. Mitch looked a little disappointed when he saw that she was wearing jeans and a T-shirt underneath, but then he turned away from her, his broad shoulders tensed.

"What's wrong, Mitch?" she asked softly, afraid to touch him and yet drawn toward him at the same time. She stood close behind Mitch and wrapped her arms around his middle. "Tell me what's the matter."

He turned in her arms, and she saw hurt in his eyes, terrible, jarring hurt, and disillusionment, too. "You don't want to know," he said hoarsely.

"Yes, I do, so start talking."

Remembering all the times when Mitch had been there for her, Shay took the glass from his hand—he'd clearly had too much to drink—and set it aside. She filled the empty hot tub with warm water and flicked the switch that activated the jets beneath the surface. She took Mitch's T-shirt off over his head and then removed his shoes and his jeans, too. He was still gaping at her when she began maneuvering him toward the bubbling hot tub.

"Get in, Prescott," she said in a tough, side-of-the-mouth voice, "or it won't be pretty!"

A grin broke through the despair in Mitch's face, though just briefly, and he slid into the tub. Shay kicked off her shoes, and then stripped completely, enjoying the amazement in his eyes.

She stepped into the tub, standing behind Mitch, working the awesome tension from his shoulders with her fingers. "Talk to me, Mitch."

Haltingly, he began to tell her about his interviews with Alan Roget. Shay had read about Roget, knew that he was a vicious killer with a penchant for calling attention to himself. She listened staunchly as Mitch poured out the ugly, inhumane things he'd be expected to write about.

When Mitch turned to her, there were tears on his beard-stubbled cheeks. Shay held him, her hands moving gently up and down his heaving back, her tears flowing as freely as his.

"How can I write about this bastard?" he demanded once, in raspy horror. "It makes me sick just to think about him!"

Shay caught Mitch's strong face in her hands and held it firmly. "You have to write about him, Mitch, because there are a lot of other psychos out there and if one woman recognizes the type and stays alive because of it—just *one woman,* Mitch—it will be worth all the pain!"

"I can't do it!" Mitch roared, and then a grating sob tore itself from the depths of him. He shuddered in Shay's arms. "Dammit, I can't do it anymore!"

"Yes you can, Mitch. I'll help you."

He drew back from her, studying her face with those tormented, fatigue-shadowed eyes. "You'll what?"

"I know you don't want a relationship with me," Shay said, wondering where she'd found the strength to admit to something that had been impossible to face only an hour before. "So there won't be any strings attached."

"Strings?"

"I love you, Mitch, regardless of how you feel about me. Tonight, I'm going to drag you back from everything that's ugly and base if I have to drive you out of your mind to do it."

She held her breath and plunged under the water to pull the plug, and the water began to drain away, but neither she nor Mitch made any move to climb out of the tub. "Your therapy begins right now," Shay said.

Because of Shay, and only because of Shay, Mitch was able to fly back to Joliet for one final interview with Roget and then to return home and write about the man. It was hell, and he swore he'd never tackle a project like it again, but by Thanksgiving he'd roughed out the skeleton of a first draft.

Shay sat on her sofa with her feet tucked underneath her, reading the last chapter. The scent of the turkey Alice had cooked still hung in the air, mingling with the spicy aroma of the pumpkin pie that would be served later. Mitch tried not to watch Shay's every expression as she read, but his eyes strayed in her direction at regular intervals.

Hank, worn out by a day of celebrating, was asleep on the couch, his head resting on Shay's lap. Mitch grinned, remembering the game of Dungeons and Dragons he and the boy had played earlier.

To keep from looking at Shay again, he watched Alice, who was sitting in a rocking chair, knitting a bright red sweater. These two women and the boy made up a family Mitch wanted very much to be a part of, but he couldn't risk proposing to Shay again; their relationship was too delicate for that.

Sitting on the floor, Mitch cupped his hands behind his head and leaned back against the chair he didn't feel like sitting in, grinning when Alice caught him staring at her and winking mischievously in response.

Shay finally finished reading and set the manuscript aside. Her eyes were averted and there was a slight flush in her cheeks and Mitch sat bolt upright.

"You don't like it," he said, hating his own vulnerability to this woman's opinion.

Shay met his gaze with a level stare of her own. "You detest this guy, Mitch. The other chapters were okay, but this one is a—a vendetta."

"Of course I detest Roget! He's a murderer!"

"Your emotions have no place in the book, Mitch. You're a journalist and you've got to be objective."

Hank stirred and muttered something and Mitch thrust himself to his feet, bending to gather the little boy up in his arms. "I'll put him to bed," he said through his teeth.

Shay smiled. "My, but you take criticism well, Mr. Prescott."

Mitch carried Hank into his room, helped him out of his clothes and into bed. "I wish you were around all the time," the child said with a yawn as Mitch tucked the blankets in around him. "It's almost like having a dad."

Mitch smiled and rumpled Hank's hair with one hand. "I'm doing my best, fella," he said quietly. "I'm doing my best."

"Are you going to marry my mom?"

Mitch thought for a moment, trying to find the right words. "I hope so," he finally said.

Hank snuggled down into the covers and yawned again, his eyes closed now. "I hope so, too," he answered.

When Mitch returned to the living room he was shocked to find Shay standing on the couch, holding out a chair, lion-tamer style, and pretending to brandish a whip with one hand. "Back, back!" she cried. To Alice, she said, "There's nothing more dangerous than a writer who's just been told that his last chapter stinks!"

Mitch was having a hard time keeping a straight face. "Oh, so now it stinks, does it?"

Shay clamped her nose with two fingers and Mitch was lost. He laughed, wrested the chair from her and pulled her down off the couch and into his arms.

"I think the pie's done," Alice chimed, beating a hasty retreat into the kitchen.

Mitch kissed the bridge of Shay's nose. "You wanna know what makes me maddest of all, lady? You're right about that last chapter. Still, you could have spared my feelings."

Impishly, she pinched him with the fingers of both hands. "I ask you, did you spare my feelings when my cheeseballs bombed at the mayor's party? No. You said you wouldn't feed them to a dog!"

"Actually, I may have spoken prematurely. I met a Doberman once, in Rio, who richly deserved one."

She laughed and the sound made a sweet, lonely ache inside Mitch. He'd never wanted anything as much as he wanted to marry this woman and share his life and his bed with her. As it was, they were together only when their schedules permitted, which wasn't often. "I love you," he said.

There was a puzzled look in her wide eyes for a moment, then she stood on tiptoe to kiss his chin. "Stay with me."

"I can't and you know it," Mitch snapped, irritated. "What would we tell Hank in the morning? That we're carrying on a cheap affair?"

Her lower lip jutted out. "Is that what you think this is, Mitch?"

He held Shay closer, desperate for the feel and scent and warmth of her. "You know damned well that that isn't what I think!"

She pinched him again, her eyes dancing with mischief. "Not even after what we did in my office yesterday?" she whispered.

Heat flowed up over Mitch's chest in a flood, surging along his neck and into his face. He swatted Shay's delectable rear end, hard, with both hands. "You little vamp, are you trying to drive me crazy or what?"

She wriggled against him. "Ooo-la-la!" she teased.

"Shay!"

She was running her hands up and down his hips and his sides. He remembered the episode she had mentioned a moment before, and Halloween night, when she'd saved him from demons that had nothing to do with the thirty-first of October. "Stay with me," she said again. "We'll set the alarm and you can leave before Hank gets up."

He set her away from him. "No, dammit. No."

Shay's eyes widened with confusion and hurt as he snatched up his jacket and the copy of the new book and started toward the door. "Mitch—?"

He paused, his hand on the knob. "I'll call you tomorrow," he said, and then he opened the door and went out.

She followed him down the walk, to the front gate and as he tried to outdistance her, she broke into a run. "What's wrong?" she asked, taking hold of his sleeve and stopping him. "Tell me what's wrong!"

"We're wrong, Shay. You and I."

"You don't mean that."

"Not the way you're taking it, no." Mitch sighed and scanned the cold November sky before forcing his eyes back to her face. "We should be able to share a bed without having to orchestrate it, Shay."

She receded. "You mean, we should be married."

"You said it, I didn't. Remember that." He opened the gate, went through it and got into his car.

Alice was in the kitchen dishing up pumpkin pie. Shay had baked so much of it for her Thanksgiving customers that she couldn't face the stuff, so she poured herself a cup of coffee and sat down at the table.

"Since nobody's volunteering anything, I'll butt my nose in and ask. What's the matter now?" Alice might have looked like a mild-mannered little old lady, but she was really a storm trooper, Shay had decided, undaunted by any assignment.

"Mitch wants to get married," Shay said despondently.

"Gee, that's terrible," came the sardonic response. "The man ought to be horsewhipped."

"It could be terrible," Shay insisted sadly. "I might be just like my mother and she was—you know how she was."

"Your great-uncle Edgar was a chicken thief, but I've yet to catch you in somebody else's coop."

Shay had to chuckle. Maybe she'd have a piece of pie after all. "Your point is well taken, but the fact remains that marriage scares me to death."

Alice refused to smile; she was clearly annoyed. "Mitch Prescott is a very fine man and you're going to fool around and lose him," she fretted.

"Have some pie," Shay said.

"I've lost my appetite," Alice snapped. "Good night and I'll see myself out."

Shay stood up. "Please, don't go."

"You should have said that to your man, Shay," Alice replied, and she walked stiffly out into the living room.

Shay followed, clenching and unclenching her hands, feeling like a miserable child. "I did. He wouldn't stay with me. He didn't want Hank to wake up and find him here."

"At least one of you has some sense." Alice murmured, her exasperation fading into tenderness. "If Mitch were your husband, there wouldn't be so many logistical problems, Shay."

"I can't marry him just so we won't have to explain going to bed!"

"You can't marry him because you're afraid, yet you love him, I know you do. And he loves you." Alice sighed, poised to leave. "Take a chance, Shay. Take a chance."

"I did that once before! And the man I loved ran off with a librarian!"

"It's a damned good thing that he did, kiddo, or you might never have found yourself. Look at you. You're in business for yourself. You're strong and you're smart and you're beautiful. What in Sam Hill do you want, a written guarantee from God?"

Shay just stared at her grandmother, stuck for an answer.

"That's what I thought. Well, you'd better not hold your breath, Shay, because we don't get any guarantees in this life." With that, Alice Bretton opened the door and walked out.

Shay went to the window and watched until her grandmother was safely in her car, then returned to the kitchen and sat staring at her half-eaten piece of pumpkin pie with its dollop of whipped cream. She stuck a finger into the topping and dolefully licked at it.

Some Thanksgiving this was. Hank was asleep and Alice had gone home in a huff and Mitch . . . She didn't even want to think about Mitch.

The next day she woke up with a chest cold and had to stay home, trusting Barbara and Louise, the two women she'd hired through the Displaced Homemaker program at the college, to run the business.

Half-buried in tissue boxes and decongestants of all sorts, Shay lay on her sofa, grimly watching game shows and soap operas and trying to be civil in the face of Hank's determined attempts to nurse her back to health.

By the time he finally gave up and went out to play with his friends, Shay was in a dreadful mood. The telephone began to ring and she made her way across the room, grumbling all the way.

"Hello," she said through her nose.

The response was a rich masculine chuckle. "Good Lord," Mitch marveled. "What's the matter with you?"

"I'm thick," Shay answered with dignity.

He laughed. "I would describe you as thin."

"Thick ath in not well," Shay labored to say.

"I'll be over in ten minutes."

Before Shay could protest that plan, Mitch had hung up. Her head pounding, she stumbled back to the couch and huddled under the afghan she'd crocheted during her earth-mother phase. She coughed and pulled the cover up over her head.

It would save the paramedics the trouble.

Chapter Thirteen

The two small shops on the first floor of Shay's building were all decorated for Christmas. She marveled at the industry of their proprietors; Jenna and Betty must have worked all of Thanksgiving weekend to assemble such grandeur, she thought.

Though her own office and kitchen were, of course, on the first floor, too, Shay climbed the stairs to see if Alice and the woman who owned the candle shop had followed suit. They had.

Shay crammed her hands into the pockets of her coat and went downstairs by the back way, feeling a little guilty because she hadn't put out so much as a sprig of holly.

Both Barbara and Louise were busy in the huge kitchen, with its big tables and commercial refrigerators. Shay watched them for a few moments, unnoticed, trying to imagine what their lives had been like.

Barbara, a plump woman with beautifully coiffed hair, was rolling out dough for an order of quiche. She had signed up for the Displaced Homemaker program at the college after her husband of twenty-eight years had divorced her for another woman. Louise, a small and perpetually smiling blonde, had lost her husband in a car accident a year before. She, like Barbara, had never held a paying job in her life, and yet she'd been faced with the prospect of earning a living.

Inwardly, Shay sighed. These two women had given their best to their marriages, and where had it gotten them? They had been betrayed, abandoned.

At that moment Barbara spotted her and smiled. "Good morning, Ms. Kendall. Feeling better?"

The inside of Shay's chest still felt raw and hollow, while her sinuses were stuffed, but the worst was past. Mitch had coddled her shamefully. "Yes," she said. "Yes, I feel better."

"You look like you dragged yourself down here," Louise observed in her forthright way. "Why don't you go home and rest? We can manage things on this end."

Shay looked upon the two women with admiration. Okay, so they were "displaced homemakers," but they were also survivors. They had tallied what skills they had—neither was a stranger to cooking for a crowd—and they'd gone out and found a market for what they knew. "I've got some book work to do in the office," she said in reply to Louise's well-meant suggestion. "But it probably would be better if you two handled the cooking today."

"I could make the deliveries, too," Barbara ventured.

I must look like I'm on my last legs, Shay thought. She nodded and went into her small office, closing the door behind her.

Her desk was piled with telephone messages, bills from food suppliers, catalogs offering fancy ice molds and serving dishes. She sighed as she sat down in her chair. She had her own business now, and she was keeping her head above water financially, which was something in the first year, so where was all the delight, all the fulfillment, all the pride of accomplishment?

Barbara and Louise were laughing in the kitchen, their voices ringing. They didn't sound very displaced to Shay. They sounded happy.

Shay opened a ledger and tried to concentrate on debits and credits, but her mind kept straying back to those two women in the kitchen. She had expected to pity them; instead she found herself envying them. Why was that?

She tapped the eraser end of her pencil against her chin. She guessed she'd qualified as a "displaced homemaker" herself, after Eliott had left her, and she'd landed on her feet, like Barbara and Louise, but she didn't remember laughing the way they were laughing now. She remembered fear and uncertainty and a constant struggle, and she remembered leaving Hank with a baby-sitter on cold winter mornings when she would have given anything to stay home and take care of him herself.

Shay sighed again, laying down her pencil. That was it, that was what she envied. For all the heartache they'd suffered in recent months, Louise and Barbara had had their time with their children. They'd been there for the first giggle, the first step, the first word.

Resolutely, Shay took up her pencil again and forced her eyes to the neat columns written in the ledger. There was no point in bemoaning such things now; she was a career woman, whether she liked it or not. And on that cold, windy November day, she didn't like it very much.

At noon Alice breezed in with chicken sandwiches from the deli down the street, her cheeks pink from the cold weather. The two women chatted about inconsequential things as they ate, and then Alice went back to her yarn shop upstairs.

Shay marveled at the woman's energy, at the same time wondering what had happened to her own. She finished balancing the books and then went into the kitchen to help Louise and Barbara box fragrant crab quiche for delivery. Once the boxes had been loaded into the back of her new station wagon, Shay confessed that she didn't think she could make it through the rest of the day and her helpers promised to take up the slack.

She delivered the quiche to the home of a prominent surgeon and his wife and then drove around aimlessly, not wanting to work, not wanting to go back to her empty house. Finally, in desperation, she went to Reese Motors to say hello to Ivy.

The office was in an uproar. Marvin was about to make another commercial and Ivy was simultaneously going over an invoice with a salesman and sparring with Richard Barrett. It gave Shay a pang to see that she'd been so easily replaced.

She would have sneaked out without speaking to Ivy at all if her friend hadn't spotted her and called out, "Shay, wait. I need to talk to you about the wedding."

Ivy got rid of the salesman and Richard in record time and all but dragged Shay into her office. It was disturbingly neat, that office.

"How have you been, Shay? Good heavens, I haven't seen you in ages!"

"I've been . . . fine."

Ivy's gaze was level. "You don't look fine. Is everything okay?"

"Please don't start, Ivy. I get enough analysis from Mitch and Alice."

Ivy grinned and lifted both hands, palms out. "Say no more." She sat down in the chair behind the desk and Shay took a seat on the sofa and it all seemed strange. It was amazing that a person could jog along in the same rut for six years and then suddenly find herself living a whole different life. "When can you work in a fitting for your dress?"

Shay stared blankly for a moment and then realized that Ivy was talking about the gown she would wear as a bridesmaid in her friend's wedding. "Flexibility is my middle name," she said awkwardly. "Name a date."

"How about tomorrow night, at my apartment? Bring Hank and Alice and we'll have supper after the sewing fairies close their little tufted boxes and steal away into the night."

Shay smiled, hoping that she didn't look forlorn. "I think I can collar Hank for the occasion, but Alice has a big date with a knitting-needle salesman."

That brought a grin from Ivy, though her eyes were serious. It was obvious that she wanted to ask how things were going with Mitch. Shay was grateful that she didn't. "How's the catering business?"

"Hectic," Shay replied without thinking. She felt foolish, sitting there in Ivy's office when she should have been in her own, working. "Do you like your new job?"

Ivy smiled pensively. "Most of the time, I thrive on it."

"And the rest of the time?"

Ivy glanced toward the office door, as if to make certain that it was tightly closed, leaned forward and whispered, "Shay, I think—I think—"

"What, Ivy?"

"I think I'm pregnant," Ivy answered in a low rush of words, and it was impossible to tell whether she was happy or not.

Shay knew what *she* felt, and that was plain, old-fashioned envy. "Have you discussed this with Todd?"

Ivy nodded. "He's thrilled."

"Are you thrilled, Ivy?"

"Yes, but I'm not looking forward to telling my mother. She'll have a fit, because of the white dress and everything."

I should have such a problem, Shay thought. "Don't worry about your mother, Ivy. Just enjoy the wedding and take things as they come."

Ivy started to say something but the telephone on her desk began to buzz. Shay mouthed a goodbye and left, feeling even more bereft than she had before she'd arrived. Her life was in limbo and she didn't know which way to turn or how to go on. She wanted to go to Mitch, but that would have been a weak thing to do, so she drove around until it was time for Hank to get out of school.

She brightened as she drew the station wagon to a stop in front of her son's school. He'd be surprised to see her, and they'd go out for hamburgers and maybe an early movie, just the two of them. Shay had it all planned out.

Only Hank scowled at her and got into the car grudgingly, his eyes averted.

"I'm glad to see you, too," Shay said. "What's the problem, tiger?"

"Nothin'."

Shay shut off the car's engine and turned to her son. She moved to ruffle Hank's hair, but he pulled away. "You're mad at me, aren't you?"

He flung her a defiant look. "Yes. You found out about your dad, but you won't tell me anything about mine!"

Shay shrank back a bit, stunned by the force of the little boy's rage. "I didn't think you were ready," she said lamely.

"I wonder about him all the time and there's nobody to tell me! It isn't fair, Mom!"

Shay closed her eyes for a moment, trying to gather strength. Hank was right. Keeping him in the dark about Eliott had not been fair. Hadn't she been angry with Rosamond for not telling her about Robert Bretton? "I'll tell you everything you want to know."

Over take-out food and the few photographs Shay had kept of Eliott, she told Hank the whole story. She told him, as kindly as she could, about the stealing and about the librarian and she ached at the hurt she saw in her son's eyes.

Hank listened in stony silence and when Shay had finished talking, he snatched up one of the snapshots of his father and went out into the backyard to sit disconsolately at the picnic table. It was cold out there, and windy, and Shay had all she could do not to go out and drag her son back inside.

Presently, he came in on his own, his small shoulders slumped, his eyes averted. Shay, conscious of his dignity, did not speak or move to touch him.

"I'll take my bath now, I guess," he said.

"Okay," Shay replied, looking out the window so that she could hide the expression on her face. The picture of Eliott was blowing across the surface of the picnic table in pieces.

At breakfast the next morning, Hank was in better spirits and Shay blessed the resiliency of children. In fact, she tried to emulate it.

She was humming when she got to the office and, just to give the day a little pizzazz, she went into the Christmas-ornament shop on the first floor and bought a fancy cornhusk wreath for the reception room. Clydesdale was positioned in the curve of the bay windows, and Shay hung the wreath on his head. "Hail, Caesar," she said, before going off to find a hammer and a nail.

The entire day went well and Shay was feeling better than she had in days when she got home. Hank was there, idly pounding one fist into his baseball glove and watching Sally, his baby-sitter, paint her toenails.

"Spruce up, fella," Shay said brightly. "We're due at Ivy's place for supper in an hour."

Hank's freckled face twisted into a grimace, then brightened. "Is Mitch going to be there?"

"I don't know. Why don't you call Ivy and ask her?"

The baby-sitter picked up a blow dryer, switched it on and aimed it at her toes. The roar drove Hank to make his call from the kitchen.

By the time Sally had dried her toenails and gone home, Shay was through with her shower and wrapped in her bathrobe, carefully applying fresh mascara.

Sensing Hank's presence behind her, she asked, "Well? Is Mitch going to be there?"

Hank was silent for so long that Shay finally turned to look at him, mascara wand poised in midair. His lower lip was quivering and everything inside Shay leaped with alarm.

"He's bringing a stupid girl!" Hank wailed.

Shay swallowed. "A girl?"

Hank nodded. "I called him up and told him off! I told him *you* were supposed to be his girl!"

"Oh, Lord," Shay breathed, closing her eyes for a moment. "Hank, you shouldn't have done that. You had no right."

"I don't care!" Hank shouted. "He's just like my dad! He's a creep!"

"Hank!"

Hank stormed into his bedroom and slammed the door and Shay knew it was useless to talk to him before he'd had a chance to calm down. She went into the living room and tried to make sense of what was happening.

Mitch and a girl? There had to be some misunderstanding. There had to be.

There was. Fifteen minutes after Hank's outburst, there came a knock at the door. Shay opened it to find Mitch standing on the porch, a small, brown-eyed girl huddling shyly against his side. "This," he said, "is the other woman."

Shay smiled and stepped back. She hoped her relief didn't show. "You must be Kelly," she said to the child, helping her out of her coat.

Kelly nodded solemnly. "I'm seven," she said.

"Where, may I ask," Mitch drawled, "is the staunch defender of your honor as a woman?"

"In his room," Shay answered, and as Mitch strode off to knock at Hank's door, she offered Kelly her hand. "Would you like a cup of cocoa?"

"Yes, please." Kelly's dark eyes made a stunning contrast to her pale hair and they moved from side to side as Shay led her toward the kitchen. "Daddy said you had a real carousel horse," she said. "I don't see him around, though."

Shay hid a smile. "I keep him at my office. We could stop there later, if you want."

"I'd like that, thank you." Kelly settled herself at the table and Shay felt a pang as she put milk on to heat for the cocoa. Her mother must be beautiful, she thought.

In a few minutes Mitch appeared in the doorway with a sheepish and somewhat sullen Hank at his side. "Another domestic crisis averted," muttered the man.

"I don't wanna go anywhere with any stupid girl," added the boy.

"I spoke too soon," Mitch said.

"Hank Kendall," Shay warned, "you go to your room, this instant!"

Kelly smoothed the skirts of her little dress. "I'm not a stupid girl," she threw out, just loud enough for a retreating Hank to hear.

"Is she always this good?" Shay whispered once Kelly had finished her cocoa and gone off to the living room to sit quietly on the couch and thumb through a copy of *House Beautiful.*

Mitch shook his head. "I'm still a novelty," he answered, trapping Shay neatly against the kitchen counter and bending to steal one mischievous kiss. "She's only staying a few days, Reba and her husband are attending some conference in Seattle." Liking the taste of the first kiss, he gave her another. "Hank's pretty upset, isn't he?"

Shay nodded. "I told him about Eliott."

Mitch's hand was in Shay's hair, his thumb tracing the rim of her ear. "You did the right thing, princess. He's going to need some time to come to terms with what happened, that's all."

"You were remarkably patient with him."

Mitch kissed her again. "I'm a remarkably patient man." His voice dropped to a whisper. "But I'd sure like to take you to bed right now, lady."

Shay trembled, needing Mitch and knowing that her need would have to be denied. "I'd sure like to go," she replied honestly.

Mitch laughed and nuzzled her neck once. "I'll try to arrange something," he said, and then they coaxed Hank out of his room and went to Ivy's apartment for the evening.

Mitch called Shay at the office first thing the next morning. "Keep the weekend open," he said. "I'm going to take you somewhere private and love you until you're crazy."

A hot, anticipatory shiver went through Shay. "What about the kids? Where would we—"

"Reba is picking Kelly up tomorrow night. Maybe Hank could stay with Alice."

"Well . . ."

"Ask her, Shay. You're talking to a desperate man, a man consumed with lust."

Shay laughed. "I'll check with Alice and call you back."

Alice asked no questions. She simply agreed to keep Hank for the weekend and returned to the group of knitters gathered at the back of the shop.

The rest of that week crept by, even though Shay was busy day and night. She didn't see Mitch at all, but he managed to keep her blood at an embarrassing simmer by calling her at intervals and making scandalous promises.

Finally, Friday afternoon arrived. Shay left the office early, picked Hank up at school and brought him back to Alice's shop.

Alice immediately set him to work unpacking a new shipment of yarn. "You just go along, dear," she whispered, half pushing Shay out through the shop's open door and into the hallway. "Hank and I will be fine."

Shay pulled a crumpled piece of paper from her coat pocket and handed it to Alice. "This is a telephone number, where you can reach us, er, me."

Alice glanced at the number, which constituted the sum total of what Shay knew about where she would be that weekend, nodded her head and tucked the paper into the pocket of her apron. "Have a lovely time, dear," she said, dismissing Shay with a wave of one hand.

Because Shay had to leave the station wagon with Barbara and Louise so that they could make deliveries, Mitch picked her up in front of the building. She felt like a fool, standing there on the front steps with her suitcase at her feet.

"I didn't even know what clothes to pack!" she snapped once she'd gotten into Mitch's car and fastened her seatbelt.

"You probably won't need any," he replied.

Their destination turned out to be a log cabin in the foothills of the Olympics. There was smoke curling from the stone chimney and lights glowed at the windows. Pine trees towered behind the small house, scenting the crisp evening air, and among them were maples and elms, a few bright orange leaves still clinging to their branches.

Mitch took the box of supplies that he'd picked up at the store down the road, and carried it to the porch step, setting it down to unlock the door. Shay took as long as she could to get her suitcase and follow.

The inside of the cabin was simplicity at its finest. The wooden floors were bare, except for a few brightly colored scatter rugs, and polished to a high shine. A fire snapped and chattered on the hearth of the rustic rock fireplace, tossing darting crimson shadows onto the tweed sofa that faced it. There was a tiny bathroom and an even tinier kitchen, where Mitch immediately busied himself putting away the food.

"Whose place is this, anyway?" Shay asked, oddly nervous considering all the times she'd been intimate with Mitch.

Mitch closed the door of the smallest refrigerator Shay had ever seen and turned to unzip her jacket and slide it off her shoulders. "It belongs to a friend of Todd's," he answered, but his mind clearly wasn't on such details. His eyes were on the third button of Shay's flannel shirt and it was a wonder that the little bit of plastic didn't melt under the heat.

"There isn't any phone. I gave Alice a number—"

"That number is for the store down the road. If anything happens, Alice will have no problem getting through to us."

Shay's arms were still in her jacket sleeves, the garment only half removed, when Mitch slipped out of his own coat and began unbuttoning her shirt. She quivered, unable to utter so much as a word of protest, as he undid the front fastening on her bra and bared her breasts.

When he touched her, with one tentative hand, she gasped with pleasure and let her head fall back, her eyes drifting shut. Mitch stroked her gently, shaping each of her breasts for his pleasure and her own, teasing her nipples until they tightened into pulsing little pebbles.

Finally he removed her jacket entirely, then her shirt and her already-dangling bra, her jeans and her shoes, her socks and, last of all, her panties. A low crooning sound came from Shay's throat as Mitch caressed every part of her with his hands, slowly, as if memorizing her shape, the texture of her flesh. One by one, he found and attended the spots where her pleasure was most easily roused.

After what seemed a dazzling eternity to Shay, he took off his clothes and they knelt, facing each other, before the fire. Now, while Mitch's hands brazenly cupped Shay's breasts, she used her own to explore him, learning each muscle in his powerful thighs with her fingers, each hollow and plane in his broad back and on his chest. At last she tangled her fingers in his hair and moved astraddle of him, catching his groan of surrender in her mouth as she kissed him and at the same time sheathing him in her warmth.

They moved slowly at first, their mouths still locked in that same kiss, their tongues mimicking the parries and thrusts of their hips.

But finally the need became too great and Shay leaned back in triumphant submission, bracing herself with her hands, her breasts swollen and heaving under the attentions of Mitch's fingers. She groaned with each slow thrust of his hips, pleaded senselessly at each lingering withdrawal.

He stopped plying her nipples with his fingers to suckle and tongue them instead and Shay was driven to madness. She threw her legs around Mitch and he shouted in a madness of his own, plunging deep.

Shay would not allow him to escape the velvety vengeance that cosseted him, rippled over him, sapped his strength. Her triumph was an elemental thing, and she shouted with the joy of it even as Mitch growled in a release of his own.

Once they'd recovered enough to rise from that rug in front of the fire, where they'd fallen in a tangle of perspiration and breathless laughter, they ate sandwiches and drank wine and then made the sofa out into a bed and made love again.

In the darkest depths of the night Shay awakened and lay listening, in perfect contentment, to the calls of the owls and the cry of some lonely, faraway beast. She felt her spirit, crumpled by the rigors of day-to-day life, unfolding like a soft cloth. She snuggled closer to Mitch and wished that they could stay there in that cabin far longer than just a weekend.

The morning was cold and the sky was a brassy blue, laced with gray clouds. Mitch and Shay consumed a hastily cooked breakfast of scrambled eggs and toast and then went outside.

They found a silver ribbon of a creek, hidden away among the trees and watched a deer dashing up a hillside, white tail bobbing. It was all so beautiful that Shay ached with the effort of trying to draw it all inside herself, to keep.

Early in the afternoon snow began to fall, drifting down in big, lazy flakes that seesawed their way to the ground. Mitch built up the fire and then came to stand behind Shay at the window, kneading her shoulders with his strong hands, his chin propped on the top of her head.

"What are you thinking, princess?"

Shay knew there would be tears in her voice and made no effort to hide them. "That two days isn't going to be enough."

"Two centuries wouldn't be enough," he agreed quietly, and his arms slid around her and tightened.

They watched the snow for hours, it seemed, and then they went back to the bed. There was no lovemaking; they were too tired for that.

When Shay was prodded awake by hunger, she sat up in bed and yawned. It was dark outside and the fire was almost out. She squinted at her watch and was shocked at the time; it was after midnight!

She prodded Mitch with one hand. "Wake up!"

He stirred briefly and then rolled over, hauling most of the covers with him and burying his face in his pillow.

Shay swatted his backside. "I said, wake up!"

He muttered something and burrowed deeper.

Disgusted, Shay scrambled out of bed and hop-danced to the window because the floor was so cold under her bare feet. The snow was deep now and it glowed in the moonlight, so white and glittery that Shay's throat went tight as she looked at it.

Her stomach rumbled and she remembered that she was hungry. She found her robe and slippers and put them on, then began ransacking the kitchen, making as much noise as she possibly could.

Mitch woke up reluctantly, grumbling and groping for his jeans. "What the—"

Shay shoved a bacon, lettuce and tomato sandwich into his hands and began wolfing down one of her own. "I challenge you to a duel, my good man," she said, eating and putting on her clothes at the same time.

"Name your weapon," Mitch muttered with a disgraceful lack of enthusiasm.

Shay stepped outside the door for a moment, wincing at the cold, and then let him have it. "Snowballs!" she shouted as the first volley struck Mitch's bare chest.

Chapter Fourteen

On Sunday morning the snow began to melt away, leaving only ragged patches of white here and there on the ground. In a like manner, Shay's dreams seemed to waste away, too. She had hoped that Mitch might propose to her again—she felt ready to accept now—but as the time for them to leave the cabin drew closer, his mood went from pensive to distant to downright sullen.

Shay watched him out of the corner of one eye as they drove past the small country store on the highway—the proprietor had been the one to build the fire and turn on the lights in the cabin before they arrived—but she didn't ask Mitch what was wrong because she thought she knew. He probably dreaded the inevitable return to the realities of the relationship as much as she did.

When Mitch reached out for the radio dial on the dashboard, Shay gently forestalled the motion.

"You've almost finished the Roget book," she threw out, to make conversation. "What's next?"

Mitch tossed one unreadable look in Shay's direction and his jawline tightened as he turned his attention back to the road. "I suppose Ivan will sift through the dregs of humanity until he finds some other scum for me to write about."

Shay stiffened. "Is that what my mother was, Mitch? The dregs of humanity?"

He cursed under his breath. "I was talking about Roget and you damned well know it. Don't bait me, Shay, because I'm not in the mood to play your games."

It was an uncomfortable reminder of the last time Mitch had accused her of playing games and Shay felt defensive. Still, she tried hard to keep her voice level. "Do you really think I want to argue with you, especially now? Especially after—"

"After what, Shay? Two days of reckless passion?" His tone was blade-sharp. Lethal. "That's our only real way of communicating, isn't it?" He paused, drew a deep, raspy breath. "I'll say one thing for us, love: we relate real well on a sexual level."

Shay was wounded and her voice sounded small and shaky when she spoke. "If you feel that way, why did you ask me to marry you?"

The brown eyes swung to her, scoured her with their anger. "I guess I lost my head," he said bluntly. Brutally. "Rest easy, sugar plum. I won't risk it again."

"Risk—"

"If you want to marry me—and I don't think you have the guts to make that kind of commitment to any man—you'll have to do the proposing. Rejection hurts, Shay, and I'm not into pain."

Shay turned her head, and the tall pine trees along the roadside seemed to whiz past the car window in a blurry rush. The terrible hurt, the three-hundred-and-sixty degree turn in Mitch's attitude, all of it was proof that she'd been wrong to expect consistent, unwavering love from a man. Why hadn't she learned? She'd watched Rosamond enter into one disastrous relationship after another. She'd nearly been destroyed by a failed marriage herself. Why in God's name hadn't she learned?

"Shay?" Mitch's voice was softer now, even gentle. But it was too late for gentleness.

She let her forehead rest against the cool, moist glass of the window, trying to calm herself. "Leave me alone."

The sleek car swung suddenly to the side of the road and came to a stomach-wrenching stop. "Shay."

She shook his hand from her shoulder, keeping her face averted. "Don't touch me, Mitch. Don't touch me."

There was a blunt sound, probably his fist striking the steering wheel or the dashboard, followed by a grating sigh. "I'm sorry. It's just that I get so frustrated. Everything was so good between us and now it's all going to hell again and I can't handle that, Shay."

"That's obvious."

She heard him sigh again, felt a jarring motion as he shifted furiously in the car seat. "Don't give any ground here, dammit. Whatever you do, don't meet me halfway!"

Shay could look at Mitch now; in fact, her pain forced her to do that. She sat up very straight in her seat, heedless of her tousled hair and the tears on her cheeks. "I've met you more than halfway, Mitch. I came up on this damned mountain with you. I shared your bed. And you turned on me."

"I didn't turn on you, Shay. I got angry. There's a difference."

"Is there?"

"Yes, dammit, there is!"

"If you truly love somebody, you don't yell at them!"

Mitch's nose was within an inch of Shay's. "You're wrong, lady, because I love you and I'm yelling at you right now! And I'll keep yelling until you hear me! I LOVE YOU! Is that coming through?"

"No!" Shay closed her eyes tightly. Memories of her mother filled her mind—Rosamond screaming, Rosamond throwing things, Rosamond driving away everyone who tried to love her. "No!"

Mitch's hands were clasping her shoulders then. "Open your eyes, Shay; look at me!"

Shay did open her eyes, but only as a reflex.

"I'm still here, aren't I? You can get mad at me, Shay, and I can get mad at you, and it's still all right. Don't you see that? It's all right."

She fell against him, burying her face in his shoulder, clinging to him with her hands. She had always been afraid of anger, in other people, in herself. And she trembled in fear of it then, even as she began to realize that Mitch was right. Getting mad was okay, it was human. It didn't have to mean the end of something good.

Presently, Mitch cupped one hand under her chin and lifted, brushing her lips with his own.

"All weekend," he said, "you've been telling me what your body wants, what it needs. Your mind and your spirit, Shay, what do they want?"

She sniffled. That one was easy. With her whole heart and soul she wanted Mitch Prescott. She wanted to laugh with him and bear his children and yes, fight with him, but she couldn't bring herself to say those things aloud. Not yet. She was still coming to terms with too many other emotions and her right to feel them.

Mitch overlooked her complete inability to answer and kissed the tip of her nose. "We'll get this right, Shay. Somehow, I'm going to get past all that pain and fear and make you trust me."

Shay swallowed hard. "I—I trust you."

He started the car again. "I'll believe that, my love, when you ask for my hand in marriage."

"It's supposed to bè the other way around, isn't it?" Shay caught her breath as the car sped onto the highway again.

"Not in this case," Mitch answered, and the subject was closed.

The boxed manuscript landed in the middle of Ivan's desk with a solid, resounding thump.

Ivan looked at the box and then up at Mitch's unyielding face. "Good Lord," the older man muttered. "You're not serious!"

"I'm serious as hell, Ivan. I'm through writing this kind of book."

Ivan gestured toward one of several chairs facing his desk. "Sit down, sit down. Let's at least talk this over. You didn't fly three thousand miles just to throw a ream of paper in my face, did you?"

Mitch ignored the invitation to sit—he'd had enough of that flying from Seattle to New York—and paced the length of Ivan's sumptuous office, pausing at the window to look down on Fifth Avenue. He thought of Shay, back home in Skyler Beach and probably up to her eyes in cheeseballs, and smiled. "I flew three thousand miles, Ivan, to tell you face-to-face that you're going to have to get yourself another Indiana Jones."

"You're older now, more settled. I can see why you wouldn't want to do the kind of research your earlier books required, but your career has taken a different course anyway, between the Rosamond Dallas biography and the Roget case. What's the real problem, Mitch?"

"A woman."

Ivan sighed. "I should have known. Don't tell me the rest of the story, let me guess. She's laid down the law. No husband of hers is going to fly all over the country chasing down leads and interviewing murderers. Am I right?"

Mitch was standing at the window, still absorbed in Fifth Avenue's pre-Christmas splendor. "You couldn't be further off base, Ivan. If it hadn't been for Shay, I wouldn't have had the stomach to write about Alan Roget."

"So she's supportive. Three cheers for her. I still don't understand why a writer would turn his back on his craft, his readers, his publishers, his—"

"I never do anything halfway, Ivan," Mitch broke in patiently. "And right now holding that relationship together takes everything I've got."

"If it's that shaky, maybe it isn't worth the trouble."

"It's worth it, Ivan."

Ivan sat back in his swivel chair, his eyes on the manuscript box in front of him. "I almost dread reading this," he observed after several moments of reflective silence. "I suppose it's just as good as your other stuff?"

"Better," Mitch said with resignation rather than pride.

Ivan was, for all his professional tenacity, a good sport. And a good friend. "This lady of yours must be something. Once the dust settles and you want to write again, you give me a call."

Mitch grinned, already at the door of Ivan's office, ready to leave. "I expect her to propose any time now," he said, enjoying the look of surprise on his agent's face. "Goodbye, Ivan, and merry Christmas."

"Bah humbug," Ivan replied as Mitch closed the door behind him.

"Doesn't anybody cook their own Christmas turkey anymore?" Shay grumbled as she read over the work schedule Barbara had just brought into her office.

Barbara was wearing a bright red apron trimmed in white lace and there was a sprig of holly in her hair. Everybody seemed to have the Christmas spirit this year. Everybody, that is, except for Shay. "If you don't mind my saying so, Ms. Kendall, most people would be glad to have so much business."

Shay sighed. "I suppose you're right."

"You don't care much for all this, do you?"

The directness of Barbara's question set Shay back on her emotional heels. "I've dreamed of owning this catering business for years!"

Barbara was undaunted. "Sometimes, we dream of something and we work and sweat and pray to get it and, when we do, we find out that it wasn't what we really wanted after all. What is it that you really want, Ms. Kendall?"

Shay blushed. Damn the woman and her uncanny perception! "I'm almost embarrassed to admit to it, in this day and age, but I'd like to be married and have babies. I'd like to have the luxury of being weak sometimes, instead of always having to be strong. I'd like to be there when my son comes home from school and I'd like to watch soap operas and vacuum rugs." Shay caught herself. Barbara would be horrified. Any modern woman would be horrified. "Aren't you sorry you asked?"

Barbara chuckled. "I was married for a long, long time, Ms. Kendall, and those were some of the things I liked best about it."

"You're not shocked?"

"Of course I'm not. You're a young woman and it's natural for you to want a man and a home and babies."

Shay was gazing toward the window. There wasn't any snow and she wanted snow. She wanted to be alone in the mountains with Mitch again. "I'm not at all like my mother," she mused in a faraway voice threaded through with a strand of pure joy. "I'm myself and I can make my own choices."

Barbara must have slipped out. When Shay looked back, she was gone.

Shay propped her chin in her hands, running over her dreams, checking each one for soundness, finding them strong. All she had to do was find the courage to act on them.

Mitch wanted a marriage proposal, did he? Well, she'd give him one he'd never forget. She reached for the telephone book and leafed through the yellow pages until she found the listings she wanted. There was no way she could put her plan into action until after Christmas, what with the business and Ivy's wedding and the general uproar of the holiday itself, but it wouldn't hurt to make a few calls.

Kelly cast one questioning look up at her mother. Reba nodded, her eyes suspiciously bright, and the child scampered through the crowd of Christmas travelers and into Mitch's arms.

He lifted her, held her close. There was no time to tell Reba that he was grateful; he and Kelly had to catch a northbound plane within minutes. He nodded and Reba nodded back. A second later, she had disappeared into the crowd.

"Look, Daddy," Kelly chimed over the standard airport hubbub, pointing to a pin on her coat. "Mommy bought me this Santa and his nose lights up when you pull the string!"

Mitch chuckled hoarsely. "Your mommy is a pretty special lady. Shall we go catch our plane?"

Kelly nodded. "Mommy already checked my suitcase and I've got my ticket right here."

Minutes later they were settled in their seats on the crowded airplane and Mitch ventured, "I know this is the first Christmas you've ever been away from your mother...."

Kelly smiled and patted his hand as though Mitch were the child and she the adult. "Don't worry, Daddy. I won't cry or anything like that. It'll be fun to be with you and be in Aunt Ivy's wedding and, besides, I get a whole other Christmas when I get back here."

The plane was taxiing down the runway and Mitch checked Kelly's seatbelt.

"I'm kind of scared," she confessed.

He took her hand.

Shay dampened her fingers on her tongue and smoothed Hank's cowlick. "I want you to be nice to Kelly," she said as the arrival of Flight 703 was announced over the airport PA system.

Hank scooted away, his dignity ruffled. "Mom, don't spit on me anymore," he complained. "I look good enough already."

Shay laughed. "I'm soooooo sorry!"

The plane landed and, after several minutes, the passengers began to stream in through the gate, most carrying brightly wrapped packages and wearing home-for-the-holiday smiles. Mitch and Kelly appeared just when Shay was beginning to worry that they'd been left behind.

Kelly pulled at a little string and the Santa Claus face pinned to her coat glowed with light. "Look, Hank!"

Hank tried his best to be blasé, but he was obviously fascinated by the plastic Santa and its flashing red nose.

"I brought you one just like it," Kelly assured him.

Shay could feel Mitch's eyes on her face, but it was a moment before she'd shored up her knees enough to risk looking into them. She wondered what he'd say when he found out that he wasn't involved with a modern woman at all, but one who wanted a time-out, who would willingly trade her career for babies and Cub Scout meetings and love in the afternoon.

Maybe he wouldn't even want a woman like that. Maybe— "Shay."

She realized that she'd been staring at Kelly's pin and made herself meet Mitch's gaze. Her throat was constricted and though her lips moved, she couldn't make a sound.

"I know my nose doesn't light up," he said with a teasing note in his voice, "but surely I'm more interesting than a plastic Santa Claus."

Shay found her voice. It was deeper than usual and full of strange little catches. "You're definitely more interesting than a plastic Santa Claus," she agreed. "But we won't make any rash statements about the nose until after Marvin and Jeannie's Christmas party."

He laughed and kissed her hungrily, but then they both remembered the children and the airport full of people and they drew apart.

"Yuk," said Hank, but his protest lacked true conviction.

Ivy's face glowed as she turned, displaying her dress for Shay. It was a beautiful white gown with tiny crystal beads stitched to the full, flowing skirt and the fitted bodice. Because this was a Christmas wedding, the hem, neckline and cuffs boasted a snowy trimming of fur.

Shay's gown, like Kelly's, was of floor-length red velvet, also trimmed with fur. In lieu of flowers, the attendants would carry matching muffs with sprigs of holly attached.

"We look beautiful!" Kelly piped out, admiring herself in the mirror of the little dressing room at the back of the church.

Ivy laughed and her joy brought a pretty apricot flush to her cheeks. "We do, don't we?"

There were still a few tinsel halos and shepherds' robes lying about from the Christmas program that had been held earlier and Shay gathered them up just for something to do to pass the time. It wasn't her wedding, but she was almost as excited and nervous as if it had been.

Ivy's mother, an attractive if somewhat icy woman, came in, followed closely by Mitch. It was obvious that Elizabeth was trying to ignore her stepson, but Shay couldn't. He looked so handsome in his dark tuxedo that she almost gasped.

He gave Shay a wink over Elizabeth's rigidly coiffed champagne-blond head and then turned his attention to Ivy. Elizabeth winced at his wolf-whistle, but Ivy glowed.

"We look beautiful, don't we, Daddy?"

Mitch crouched to look into Kelly's face. "Yes, indeed, you do."

"You shouldn't have just walked in here that way," Elizabeth fretted, speaking to Mitch but not looking at him. "They might have been dressing."

Mitch wagged a finger in her face. "Peace on earth, Elizabeth. Good will toward men."

To the surprise of everyone, Elizabeth permitted herself a faltering smile. "You are just like your father," she said. Shay hoped that Mitch had noticed the love in Elizabeth's face when she mentioned his father.

"Merry Christmas, Elizabeth," he said gently, and then he kissed Ivy's cheek and left the room.

There were tears glistening in Ivy's eyes as she looked at her mother. "Thank you, Mama," she said quietly.

"Pish-posh, all I did was speak to the man," Elizabeth replied, and then she was fussing with Ivy's skirts and straightening her veil.

Minutes later, Kelly led the way up the aisle of the candlelit church. Shay followed, smiling when she spotted Marvin and Jeannie. As she passed Alice, the old dickens winked at her.

There was a hush in the crowded sanctuary as Ivy appeared in the rear doorway, her face hidden by a veil that caught sparkles of candlelight. Mitch stood at her side, and he looked as comfortable in a tux as he did in the blue jeans and T-shirts he usually wore.

The organ struck the first chord of the wedding march and there was a rustling sound as the guests rose. Everyone else was looking at Ivy, of course, but Shay's eyes would not leave the man who would give away the bride.

For Shay, the ceremony passed in a shimmering haze. The holy words were spoken and Shay heard them in snatches, adding her own silent commentary. "For better or worse." *Let it be better.* "For richer or poorer." *No problem there. These two already have IRAs.* "In sickness and in health." *Please, they're both so beautiful.* "Till death do you part." *They'll grow old together—I want your word on that, God.* "I now pronounce you man and wife, you may kiss the bride." *My feet hurt. Is this thing almost over?*

It was over. Triumphant music filled the church and the bride and groom went down the aisle together, each with an arm around the other. Kelly followed, on cue, but the best man had to give Shay a little tug to get her in motion.

Snow was wafting slowly down from the night sky as Ivy and Todd got into their limousine and raced away toward the restaurant where their reception was being held.

Hank pulled at Shay's skirt. "Mom? If nobody's at home when Santa Claus gets there, will he still leave presents?"

Shay bent and kissed the top of his head. "Don't you worry, tiger. He'll definitely leave presents."

"That's easy for you to say," Mitch muttered into her ear. "Where did you say all that stuff was hidden?"

"On the big shelf over the cellar stairs," Shay whispered back.

"I'll meet you at the reception," Mitch said after he'd helped Shay and Alice into Shay's station wagon. Hank and Kelly were in the back seat giving voice to the visions that would later dance in their heads.

"He's tall for an elf," Alice commented as Mitch walked away and got into his own car.

A few hours later, when Hank and Kelly were both sound asleep on beds Mitch had improvised for them by putting chairs together, Ivy and Todd left the reception with the customary fanfare, the guests throwing rice, God throwing snow.

"Did you set the presents out?" Shay whispered to Mitch.

He touched the tip of her nose. "Yes. And I filled Hank's stocking."

The other wedding guests were all putting on their coats and the sight gave Shay a sad feeling. It was

Christmas eve and she wished that she could share the last magical minutes of the night with Mitch. It would have been fun to set out presents and fill stockings together, talking in Santa Claus whispers....

"I'll see you tomorrow," Mitch said gently. It seemed that he had read her thoughts, that he shared them.

After dropping Alice off at her apartment—like Mitch and Kelly, she would spend Christmas day at Shay's house—Shay ushered her sleepy son out of the car and up the front walk to the door. The porch light was burning bright and she blessed Mitch for remembering to leave it on as she rummaged through her purse for her keys.

The tinsel on the Christmas tree shimmered in the dim light as Shay passed it, and snow still wafted past the windows. She put Hank to bed and returned to the living room, switching on the small lamp on the desk.

Hank's toys had been carefully arranged under the tree, his new skateboard, his electric train, his baseball glove. His stocking, resting on the sofa because there was no mantelpiece, bulged with candy canes and jacks, rubber balls and decks of cards. Shay had shopped for all these things herself, but it seemed to her that there were a few more packages than there should have been.

She took a closer look and found that four enormous presents, all tagged with Hank's name, had been added to the loot. Smiling to herself, she shut out the light and went into her room.

Santa had visited there, too, it seemed. Her bed was heaped with gifts wrapped in silver paper and tied with gossamer ribbons. Shay's heart beat a little faster as she crept closer to the bed, feeling the wonder, the magic, that is usually reserved for children.

Some of the packages were large, and some were small. Shay shook them, one by one, and the biggest one made a whispery sound inside its box. She lifted a corner of the foil lid but couldn't see a thing.

Should she or shouldn't she?

She tried to distract herself by stacking the gifts and carrying them out to the Christmas tree. She would open her presents in the morning, she decided firmly, when Hank opened his. When Mitch and Kelly and Alice were all there to share in the fun.

Resolutely, Shay washed her face, brushed her teeth and put on her warmest flannel nightgown. She tossed back the covers and started to get into bed, only to find a tiny red stocking lying on the sheet.

She upended it and a small, black velvet box tumbled out, along with a note. Shay's fingers trembled as she opened the paper and read, "I want your body. Love, Santa."

She was smiling and crying, both at once, as she opened the velvet box. Inside it was a beautiful sapphire ring, the stone encircled by diamonds.

On impulse, she grabbed for the phone on her beside table and punched out Mitch's number. He sounded wide awake when he answered.

"It's beautiful," she said.

There was a smile in his voice. "You're beautiful," he countered.

Shay willed him to say that the ring was an engagement ring, but he didn't. She wasn't going to get out of proposing, it appeared. "I left your present with Mrs. Carraway," she said, admiring the flash of the beautiful stones. "I asked her to put it in the library, on top of the TV."

"That's intriguing," Mitch answered. "I'll get it and call you back."

Shay's heart was in her throat. In order to withstand the wait, she scampered out to the living room and snatched up the big present that had made her so curious.

Chapter Fifteen

The package was sitting on top of the TV set in the library. Mitch smiled as he picked it up and turned it over in his hands, savoring not the gift itself, but the thought of the woman who had given it. After some time, he tore away the wrapping; by the shape, he had expected a book, but he saw now that Shay's present was a videotape instead.

His lips curved into a grin. The woman was full of surprises.

He slid the tape into the videocassette recorder and pressed the proper buttons and, as he settled himself on the library couch, Shay's face loomed on the television screen. "Oh, Lord," she muttered, "I think it's going already."

Mitch chuckled.

The camera's shift from telephoto to wide angle was dizzying; Mitch felt as though he'd been flung backward through a tunnel. Shay was fully visible, standing in front of a gigantic cardboard rainbow and looking very nervous.

"I love you," Mitch mumbled to her image.

The cardboard rainbow toppled over, and Shay blushed as she bent to pick it up. "You'll have to be patient," said the screen Shay. "I rented this camera and I don't know how to work it."

He heard Alice say, off-camera, "I'll be going now. Good luck, dear." A door clicked shut.

The rainbow threatened to fall again and Shay steadied it before going on. The pace of her living room production picked up speed.

"Mitch Prescott!" she crowed so suddenly and so volubly that he started. "Do I have a deal for you!"

Mitch leaned forward on the couch because the picture on the screen seemed blurry. He told himself that the video camera must have been out of focus.

"We all know that rainbows are a symbol of hope," Shay went on with an enthusiasm that would have put Marvin Reese to shame. She thumped the rainbow in question and it toppled to the floor again; part of Shay's TV set and the end of her sofa came into view. Resolutely she wrestled the prop back into place. "But rainbows can get a bit ragged, can't they?"

Mitch almost expected a toll-free number to appear on the screen, along with an order to have his credit card information ready. He grinned and rubbed his eyes with a thumb and forefinger.

"I'm offering you a brand-new rainbow, Mitch Prescott," Shay went on, in a gentle voice. Then, suddenly, she made him jump again. "But wait!" she cried. "There's still more!"

Mitch leaned forward.

"With this rainbow—" this time she held onto it with one hand while thumping it for emphasis with the other "—you get one wife, guaranteed to love you always. Yes, that's right! Even if you get bored and go back to doing dangerous things and writing books about nasty people, this wife will still love you. She'll laugh with you, she'll cry with you, and if worse comes to worst, she'll even fold your socks. Call now, because a woman this good won't last long! She's ready to deal!"

Shay left the rainbow to its own devices and came closer to the camera, peering into the lens. "You wanted a proposal and this is it. Will you marry me, Mitch?"

Mitch was overwhelmed with a crazy tangle of emotions; one by one, he unwound them, defined them. There was love, of course; he felt a tenderness so deep that it was almost wounding. There was admiration, there was humor, there was gratitude. He knew, perhaps better than anyone else could have, what it had cost Shay to lay all her emotional cards on the table.

The screen was blank now, buzzing with static. He left the couch, pressed the rewind button on the recorder and watched the tape again, this time standing, his arms folded across his chest as if to brace himself against some tidal wave of emotion.

Shay felt downright dissolute, waking up in a mink coat, curled up around the telephone as though it were a teddy bear.

Mitch hadn't called. Surely he'd seen the tape by now, but he hadn't called.

Shay sat up and squinted at the clock on her bedside table. It was five-fifteen. No point in going back to sleep; Hank would be up and ready to rip into the presents at any moment.

She lay back on her pillows, setting the phone away from her. Her hands came to rest in the deep, lush fur of the coat and tears smarted in her eyes. Maybe Mitch didn't see her as wife material after all. Maybe she was more of a kept woman, a bird in a gilded cage.

Shay bounded off the bed, tore off the fur coat and flung it across the room. Then, in just her flannel nightgown, she padded out into the living room to turn up the thermostat and light the tree. She had just turned away from the coffeemaker when she heard Hank's first squeal of delight.

When Shay reached the living room, her son was whizzing over the linoleum on his new skateboard. She couldn't help smiling. "Hank Kendall, get off that thing!" she ordered, a mother to the end.

"I suppose we can't open presents until Grammie gets here," he threw out as he came to a crashing stop against the far wall.

"You suppose right, fella."

Hank was beaming as he left the skateboard behind to crouch in front of the tree and examine his electric train. "This is going to be a great Christmas, Mom!"

Shay leaned against the jamb of the kitchen doorway, her smile a bit shaky now. She'd bared her soul to Mitch Prescott, like a fool, and he hadn't even bothered to call. Sure, it was going to be a great Christmas. "I'll get breakfast started." She waggled a motherly finger at her son. "You content yourself with the Santa Claus things and whatever might be in your stocking, young man. No present-peeking allowed!"

The doorbell rang fifteen minutes later and Shay greeted a package-laden Alice.

"Look, Grammie!" Hank crowed, delighted, as his electric train raced around its track, whistle tooting. "Look!"

Alice laughed and rumpled her great-grandson's red-brown hair, but it was obvious that she had noticed Shay's mood. She placed her packages under the tree, took off her coat and bright blue knitted hat and joined Shay in the kitchen.

Shay was thumping dishes and pans around as she set the table for breakfast.

"What's the matter, Shay?" Alice asked. The look in her eyes indicated that she already knew the answer.

"He gave me a mink coat!" Shay exclaimed, slamming down a platter of sausage links.

"I always said that man was a waster," Alice mocked in a wry whisper.

Shay was not about to be amused. "It's some kind of sick game. I made an absolute fool of myself proposing to him—"

"I take it he's had an opportunity to watch the commercial?"

"He's had all night!" Suddenly tears began to stream down Shay's cheeks. "Oh, Alice, he's going to say no!"

Alice shook her head. "I doubt that very much, Shay. Mitch loves you."

"Then why hasn't he called? Why isn't he here?"

"He probably wants to accept in person, Shay." At the protest brewing on Shay's lips, Alice raised both hands in a command of silence. "The man has a little girl, and it *is* six o'clock on Christmas morning, you know. Give him a chance to wade through the wrapping paper, at least!"

Shay was comforted, if grudgingly so. "I still think he should have called," she muttered.

"Let Mitch have this time with his daughter, Shay," Alice said gently. "It's probably the first Christmas he's spent with Kelly since the divorce."

Chagrined, Shay nodded. "Breakfast is ready," she said.

Except for the stack of gifts Mitch had left, Santa Claus-style, on Shay's bed the night before, all the presents had been opened. The living room looked like the landscape of some strange wrapping-paper planet.

Shay was gathering up the papers and stuffing them into a garbage bag when the doorbell rang. A sense of sweet alarm surged through her as Hank left his electric train to answer.

"That stuff you gave me was really neat!" the little boy whooped, and his face glowed as Mitch lifted him up into his arms and ruffled his hair.

"I'm glad you liked it," was the quiet answer.

Kelly came shyly past her father, holding the doll that had been her gift from Shay. A beautiful, delicate fairy, complete with silvery wings and wand, the doll was well suited to its ladylike owner. "Thank you very much," the little girl said, looking up at Shay with Mitch's eyes.

Shay forgot her own nervousness and smiled at Kelly. "You're welcome, sweetheart."

Alice, who had been quietly reading a book she had received as a gift, suddenly leaped out of her rocking chair, the warmth of her smile taking in both Kelly and Hank.

"Let's go and see how that turkey of ours is coming along, shall we?"

The children followed Alice into the kitchen.

"Crafty old dickens," Mitch muttered, watching Alice's spry departing figure with a smile in his eyes.

Shay suddenly felt shy, like a teenager who has just asked a boy to a Sadie Hawkins dance. She just stood there, in the middle of a mountain range of Christmas paper, the garbage bag in one hand, stricken to silence.

Mitch seemed similarly afflicted.

Alice finally intervened. "Get on with it," she coaxed from the kitchen doorway. "I can't keep these kids interested in a turkey forever, you know!"

The spell was broken. Mitch laughed and so did Shay, but her nervousness drove her back to her paper gathering.

Mitch waded through the stuff to stop her by gripping both her wrists in his hands. "Shay."

She looked up into his face, her chin quivering, and thought that if he turned down her proposal, she'd die. She'd surely die.

"Where did you get that rainbow?" he asked softly.

Shay was incensed that he could ask such a stupid question when she was standing there in terrible suspense. "I made it myself," she finally replied through tight lips.

He pried the garbage bag from one of her hands and a wad of paper from the other. "I love you," he said.

Shay thought of the mink coat lying on her bedroom floor, the sapphire ring on her finger, the stack of elegantly wrapped gifts tucked beneath the Christmas tree. "I will not be your mistress, Mitch Prescott," she said in a firm whisper.

Puzzlement darkened his eyes to a deeper shade of brown. "My what?"

"You heard me. If we're going to be together at all, we're going to be married."

One of his hands rose to cup her face. His skin was cold from the crisp Christmas-morning weather outside, and yet his touch was unbelievably warm. "I'm ready to deal," he said, and the light in his eyes was mischievous.

Shay's heart was hammering against her rib cage. "Are you saying yes, or what?"

"Of course I'm saying yes."

Shay's relief was of such intensity that it embarrassed her, coloring her cheeks. Her eyes snapped. "It so happens, Mr. Prescott, that there are a few conditions."

"Such as?" he crooned the words, his thumb moving along Shay's jawline and setting waves of heat rolling beneath her skin.

Shay swallowed hard. "I feel so foolish."

He kissed her, just nibbling at her lips, at once calming her and exciting her in a very devastating way. "You, the rainbow mender? Foolish? Never."

"I worked very hard to start my catering business," she blurted out. There was more to say, but Shay's courage failed her.

"I understand."

Shay forced herself to go on. "I don't think you do, Mitch. I—I thought it was what I wanted, but—"

Mitch arched one eyebrow. "But?"

"But it isn't. Not for now, anyway. Mitch, I want to take a time-out. I want to let Barbara and Louise run the business for a while. For now, I'd just like to be your wife and Hank's mother."

His lips twitched slightly. "Why was that so hard to say?" he asked, and he was holding Shay close now, so close that she could feel the beat of his heart through his coat.

"I guess I thought you were going to be horrified, or something," Shay mused aloud. "Most women of to-day..."

"You are not 'most women,' Shay." He cupped his hand under her chin and made her look at him. "I hope you kept that cardboard rainbow."

Shay was puzzled. "It's in the utility room. Why would you want a paper rainbow?"

Mitch ran a finger along her jawline again, setting her aquiver. "For the rainy days, Shay. There will be a few of those, you know."

She understood then, and she smiled. "We'll have our quarrels, I suppose."

"Quarrels? We'll have wars, Shay." The brown eyes twinkled. "But we'll have a good time negotiating the peace treaties."

Shay laughed and snuggled closer to him. "Ummm. I like the sound of that."

He swatted her bottom with one hand. "You would, you shameless vixen!" His whisper sent an aching heat all through her, and so did his gentle nip at her ear-lobe.

The tropical sun was hot, shimmering on the white sands of the secluded Mexican beach, dancing golden on water of so keen a blue that just looking at it made Shay's breath catch in her throat.

"Mitch?"

He was sitting on the small terrace outside their hotel room, his feet up on the railing, a man with five long minutes of marriage behind him. He looked back over one shoulder and laughed. "It's a little warm for that, isn't it?"

Shay ran her hands down the front of the mink coat he'd given her for Christmas. "It's New Year's day," she answered. "That means it's cold at home."

"Your logic, once again, escapes me."

Gulls and other seabirds squawked in the silence; it was the time of siesta and most of Mexico seemed to be asleep. Shay yawned and opened her coat.

Mitch, the sophisticate, the man of adventure, actually gasped. His eyes moved over Shay's naked body with quiet hunger, leaving a fever in their wake. He rose slowly from his chair and came toward her, pressing her back into the shadowy coolness of their room. "Mrs. Prescott," he muttered. "You are about to have the loving of your life."

She slid the coat back from her shoulders, allowed it to slip sensuously down her back and arms to the floor, where it lay in a lush, sumptuous pool. "Call now," she purred. "A wife this good can't last long."

As if bewitched, Mitch stepped closer. His throat moved, but he seemed incapable of anything more than the guttural growl he gave when she began unbuttoning his shirt.

Shay undressed her husband very slowly, pausing now and then to touch a taut masculine nipple with the tip of her tongue or tangle a finger in the hair on his chest. His groans of pleasure excited her to greater devilment.

Mitch bore her mischief as long as he could, then, with gentle force, he pressed her to the bed. He lay beside her for a time, caressing her breasts, her stomach, her thighs and even the backs of her knees. And when he had set her afire, he began kissing all those same places.

Shay's triumph became need; she twisted and tossed on the satin comforter that covered their marriage bed, she whimpered as he loved her, tasted her, tormented her.

Only when she pleaded did he take her.

Nine months and ten minutes later, as Mitch liked to say, Robert Mitchell Prescott was born.

Epilogue

It had been one hell of a fight; the rafters were still shaking.

Glumly, Mitch climbed the steps leading to the attic and opened the door. He flipped a switch and the huge room was bathed in light.

There were cobwebs everywhere and for a moment Mitch hesitated, then grew angry all over again.

It wasn't as though he intended to do anything really dangerous, after all. He wouldn't be tangling with Nazis or Klan members or hit men. This book was about racecar drivers, dammit!

He sat down on the top step, his chin in his hands. Okay, so he'd told Shay that he was through writing adventure books and now he was about to go back on his word, however indirectly. Hadn't she told him herself that she'd love him even if he did that?

Mitch gave a long sigh. He loved Shay, needed her, depended on her in more ways than he dared to admit. And yet he'd just spent half an hour hollering at her, and she'd hollered back, with typical spirit.

Mitch was glad that Hank and the baby were with Alice that day. The uproar might have traumatized them both.

After a long time, he stood up and went into the attic.

Shay sat in one corner of the library sofa, her eyes puffy from crying, her throat raw. She couldn't believe that she'd yelled those awful things at Mitch. He was her husband, the father of her son, and she loved him more than she had on her wedding day, more with every passing minute.

She hugged herself. She'd known that Mitch would eventually want to write again, once the scars on his spirit had had time to heal. She'd known it, even without being warned by both Alice and Ivan, Mitch's agent.

Shay snatched a tissue from the box on her lap and blew her nose. Loudly. She supposed she should be grateful that Mitch was only planning to drive race-cars; knowing him, he might have parachuted into Central America or slipped past the Iron Curtain into some country where women wore frumpy scarves and men talked in Slavic grunts.

She rested her hands on her still-flat stomach, where a new baby was growing. She'd wanted to tell Mitch, use it to hold him to a quiet life of building condominiums with Todd Simmons, but that wouldn't have been fair. She sniffled again and reached for another tissue.

If she insisted that Mitch stay, he would give in. Shay knew that. But he would be miserable and there would be more fights. Gradually the great love they shared would be worn away.

The telephone rang and, because it was Mrs. Carraway's day off, Shay answered. The voice on the other end of the line was Garrett's.

"Hi'ya, Amazon," he said.

Shay burst into tears.

"What is it?" Garrett asked softly when the spate of grief was over.

Feeling like an absolute fool, Shay explained. The book about Rosamond had been published under Mitch's real name, so that much of his career was no longer a secret.

Garrett waited until Shay had told him all her fears of seeing Mitch crash in a burning racecar on some faraway track and there was a gentle reprimand in his voice when he spoke. "If you wanted to go back to your catering business, you'd do it, wouldn't you, even if it made Mitch mad?"

"That's hardly the same thing! I made cheeseballs, Garrett. I didn't race around some speedway, taking my life in my hands!"

"It *is* the same thing, Shay."

Shay dabbed at her face with a wad of tissue. "I know, I know. But I love him, Garrett."

"Enough to let him be himself?"

"Yes," Shay answered after a long time. "But that doesn't mean I have to like it."

Garrett chuckled. "I guess I called at a bad time. I'll get back to you later, sweetheart. Keep the faith."

Shay might have protested, but for the strange bumping-and-thumping sound coming from the stairway. "If you were calling about this year's camping trip, Hank is all for it."

Garrett promised to call again and hung up.

"Shay?"

She turned on the sofa to see Mitch leaning against one side of the library doorway. Despite his attempt at nonchalance, he looked wan and haggard and Shay felt a painful tightening in her heart. But fear for him made her voice cool. "Yes?"

"I won't go if it's that important to you. I'll write a novel or something."

Shay felt all broken and raw inside. "You'll only be racing for two or three weeks, won't you? Actually driving the cars, I mean?"

She thought she saw hope leap in the depths of his dark, dark eyes. "Three weeks at the most," he promised hoarsely.

"I'll hate every minute of it. I love you, Mitch."

He disappeared around the corner, came back in a moment dragging a very large and very dusty cardboard rainbow. A shower of glued-on glitter fell from the colorful arch as Mitch pulled it across the room and propped it against his desk.

"I think this is one of those rainy days we talked about," he said.

Shay felt tears sting her eyes. It was late July and the sun was shining, but Mitch was right. She held out her arms to him and he came to her, drawing her close, burying his face in the warm curve of her neck.

"I love you," he said.

Shay tangled the fingers of one hand in his hair. It was dusty from his foraging expedition in the attic. "And I love you. Too much to keep you here if that's not what you want."

"You could go with me." His hand was working its way under her sweater, cupping one breast, not to give passion but to take comfort.

"Of course I'll go."

Mitch lifted his face from her neck, let his forehead rest against hers. His fingers continued to caress her breast, after dislodging her bra. "Thank you," he said.

"I'd better get at least a dedication out of this," Shay warned. "I don't exactly enjoy standing around race-tracks with my heart stuffed into my sinuses, you know."

Mitch had found her nipple and his fingers shaped it gently. "My other books were dedicated to you. Why would this one be different?"

Shay was kneeling on the sofa now, her forehead still touching Mitch's. He had dedicated her mother's book to her, and the one about Alan Roget, too. She couldn't for the life of her remember what he'd said in those dedications, though. She groaned softly with the pleasure he could so easily arouse in her. "Is this the part where we work out a treaty?"

Mitch chuckled. "Yes." Deftly, he unfastened the catch of her bra, freeing her breasts, catching first one and then the other in the warm, teasing strength of his hand. With his other hand, he caressed her.

"Clearly, sir," she managed to say. "It isn't a treaty you want, but a full surrender."

He lifted her sweater high enough to bare one of her breasts and bent to take a tantalizing nip at its throbbing peak. "How astute you are," he muttered, his breath warm against her flesh.

Shay trembled. They were, after all, in the library. It was the middle of the day and anyone could walk in. "Mitch," she protested. "Alice—the kids—"

Mitch circled her nipple with the tip of his tongue, then got up to close and lock the library doors.

Silhouette Special Edition

COMING NEXT MONTH

SOMETHING ABOUT SUMMER—Linda Shaw
State Prosecutor Summer MacLean didn't know what to do when she
found herself handcuffed to a suspect determined to prove he was
innocent . . . and who happened to look like her late husband.

EQUAL SHARES—Sondra Stanford
When Shannon Edwards inherited fifty-one percent of a troubled
business, she went to check it out. She expected a problem, but not the
sexiest man alive . . . her partner.

ALMOST FOREVER—Linda Howard
Max Conroy was buying out the company where Claire worked, and used
her to get the vital information. What he didn't figure on was falling in
love.

MATCHED PAIR—Carole Halston
The handsome gambler and the glamorous sophisticate met across the
blackjack table, and it was passion at first sight. Neither realized they were
living a fantasy that could keep them apart.

SILVER THAW—Natalie Bishop
Mallory owned prize Christmas trees, but had no one to market them. The
only man willing to help her was the man who had once sworn he
loved her.

EMERALD LOVE, SAPPHIRE DREAMS—Monica Barrie
Pres Wyman had been the school nerd. But when Megan Teal hired him to
help her salvage a sunken galleon, she found the erstwhile nerd had
become a living Adonis.

AVAILABLE THIS MONTH:

**MISTY MORNINGS, MAGIC
NIGHTS**
Ada Steward

SWEET PROMISE
Ginna Gray

SUMMER'S STORM
Patti Beckman

WHITE LACE AND PROMISES
Debbie Macomber

SULLIVAN vs. SULLIVAN
Jillian Blake

RAGGED RAINBOWS
Linda Lael Miller

FOUR UNIQUE SERIES
FOR EVERY WOMAN YOU ARE . . .

Silhouette Romance

Heartwarming romances that will make you
laugh and cry as they bring you all the wonder
and magic of falling in love.

6 titles
per month

Silhouette Special Edition

Expanded romances written with emotion and
heightened romantic tension to ensure
powerful stories. A rare blend of passion and
dramatic realism.

6 titles
per month

Silhouette Desire

Believable, sensuous, compelling—and
above all, romantic—these stories deliver
the promise of love, the guarantee
of satisfaction.

6 titles
per month

Silhouette Intimate Moments

Love stories that entice; longer, more
sensuous romances filled with adventure,
suspense, glamour and melodrama.

4 titles
per month